The questio... ...the air like the aftershock of an explosion. Aleta had never been angrier in her life.

The question had cut to the core, to the part within her that had never known intimacy and yet longed for it.

"I don't think that question has anything to do with security," she said quietly. "And, if you ask me one more personal question as offensive as that, I will leave."

Giancarlo interrupted. "I already know the answer."

"Oh, really?" Aleta asked.

"I can see it in your eyes."

Her mouth flew open, but the nasty retorts she wanted to make didn't come out. She wanted to tell him that everything she had read about him was true. He was rude, aloof, arrogant, disdainful, cold. And she wanted to prove him wrong... even if he wasn't.

Dear Reader,

What a fabulous lineup we have this month at Silhouette Romance. We've got so many treats in store for you that it's hard to know where to begin! Let's start with our WRITTEN IN THE STARS selection. Each month in 1992, we're proud to present a Silhouette Romance novel that focuses on the hero and his astrological sign. This month we're featuring the charming, handsome Libra man in Tracy Sinclair's *Anything But Marriage*.

Making his appearance this month is another one of our FABULOUS FATHERS. This delightful new series celebrates the hero as father, and the hero of Toni Collins's *Letters from Home* is a very special father, indeed.

To round out the month, we have warm, wonderful love stories from Pepper Adams, Geeta Kingsley, Vivian Leiber, and as an added treat, we have Silhouette Romance's first PREMIERE author, Patricia Thayer. PREMIERE is a Silhouette special event to showcase bright, new talent.

In the months to come, watch for Silhouette Romance novels by many more of your favorite authors, including Diana Palmer, Annette Broadrick and Marie Ferrarella.

The Silhouette Romance authors and editors love to hear from readers, and we'd especially love to hear from *you*.

Happy reading from all of us at Silhouette!

Valerie Susan Hayward
Senior Editor

HER OWN
PRINCE CHARMING
Vivian Leiber

Silhouette
ROMANCE™

Published by Silhouette Books New York

America's Publisher of Contemporary Romance

To Wendy and Valerie,
thanks for making my own fairy tale come true.

SILHOUETTE BOOKS
300 E. 42nd St., New York, N.Y. 10017

HER OWN PRINCE CHARMING

ISBN: 0-373-08896-5

First Silhouette Books printing October 1992

Printed in the U.S.A.

Books by Vivian Leiber

Silhouette Romance

Casey's Flyboy #822
Goody Two-Shoes #871
Her Own Prince Charming #896

VIVIAN LEIBER

Although she had always wanted to be a writer, Vivian Leiber went to law school, thinking it would be more "practical." She might never have pursued her dream of writing had it not been for an insistent pile of laundry, an important trial brief and a toddler who couldn't sleep—all demanding her attention at eleven-thirty one night. Suddenly Vivian realized she couldn't have it all—and she wasn't even sure she wanted "it," anyway!

"With a husband, two stepchildren and a two-year-old son to take care of, I was stretched to the limit," she explains.

When she thought about what was most important to her, it was family and writing—in that order. Quitting her job—trading her gray power suits for jeans and her briefcase for a laptop computer—Vivian now has time for her family (especially her son, who is now four), her friends, her writing and even sleep. With three novels published with Silhouette and more to come, she hopes that she's starting off a lifelong friendship—with her readers!

By Command
of
Her Royal Majesty
Queen Marianya of the Principality of Monticello
You are invited to attend
the wedding of
His Royal Highness
Prince Giancarlo
to
Miss Aleta Clayton

On the first Friday of the Month of May
at ten o'clock
At the Cathedral
of
Saint Joseph Our Protector

Chapter One

...Meanwhile, Queen Marianya of Monticello is reported to be quite disturbed at Prince Giancarlo's playboy ways. While the bad-boy prince skied and frolicked in the company of several jet-set ladies at Gstaad, Switzerland, over the holidays, the queen reportedly met with her cabinet to discuss his unmarried state. Under a 1456 treaty with Spain, the principality of Monticello reverts back to Spain unless Giancarlo's heir is produced within the next two years—before his thirty-fifth birthday. The queen, said by our *Snoop* Palace insider to be ready to abdicate in favor of her son, is anxious for speedy nuptials and the birth of a new heir. Further complicating matters is that, according to Monticello custom, Giancarlo's future bride must come from one of five noble families of the principality—all descendants of five knights whose outstanding valor during Monticello's 1456 war with Spain are still celebrated.

Monticello, which maintains its idyllic agricultural life with the zillions it makes from tourism and international banking, has been abuzz since our recent *Snoop* story regarding just a few of the high-level noble gal pals linked to the prince....

Aleta Clayton scanned the pictures accompanying the *International Snoop* article. Prince Giancarlo of Monticello had been caught by diligent paparazzi during a snowball fight with two young blondes. The trio's brilliantly colored ski outfits, the crisp outline of snow and pine, the backdrop of a luxurious ski lodge were a striking contrast to the gray Chicago day that lurked outside the window of the cramped office she shared with three other bookkeepers for the McCormick Industrial Supply Company.

The writers of the *Snoop* article seemed to think that Prince Giancarlo was spoiled, petulant, demanding, aloof and prone to temper tantrums—although, for a few months last year, after Prince Giancarlo had saved a woman drowning off the Mediterranean coast of Monticello, the *International Snoop* had thought he was strong, sensitive, charming, shy and terribly, terribly misunderstood. Then, as was so often his habit, the prince had punched a *Snoop* photographer who fell with his camera from a tree overlooking the prince's garden terrace....

What a life! Aleta thought, fantasizing about the handsome prince as she sat at her desk. She fingered the cool, smooth surface of the pendant she wore, a pendant her mother had given her, which depicted the 1456 battle between the five illustrious Monticello knights and the Spanish *soldado*. Aleta's was an unconscious gesture of hope that some of the present-day Monticello glamour and fun would wear off onto her own life.

I wouldn't mind being a princess, she dreamed, transposing herself momentarily into the series of *Snoop*'s candid shots of Prince Giancarlo and his friends at a nightclub. Aleta could almost feel the brush of a soft velvet evening gown against her skin, the tickling of champagne bubbles on her throat, the weight of diamonds on her wrist, the feel of the prince's black curls as she steadied herself against him while he whispered conspiratorially in her ear.

After all, Aleta thought, *in my fantasy life I can have even the most outlandish, improbable things happen— like the most handsome prince in the world in love.*

With me.

An ordinary bookkeeper from Chicago.

One of thousands of women who are shut away each morning in their offices.

My life would be a lot different if I were a princess.

A lot more fun, a lot more glamorous, a lot more wonderful.

With Prince Giancarlo in love with me, whispering the words of romance in my ear.

"Are those invoices ready to send out?" An angry voice growled.

Aleta startled to see Mr. McCormick standing in front of her desk. A quick glance at the overhead clock told her she was still on coffee break so she shouldn't feel guilty about reading a magazine.

But when had Mr. McCormick ever recognized the morning coffee break when he shouted about those payroll deduction sheets and invoices? She hastily folded up the *International Snoop* and shoved it underneath her desk into her bag.

"I'm sorry, Mr. McCormick," she said and forced herself to look directly at the imposing man. "What were you asking?"

Maggie, Aleta's best friend, rolled her eyes from behind their boss as an expression of solidarity. Her other two office mates, Rhoda and Carla, though sympathetic, hid their faces in their piles of orders, payroll deduction sheets and receipts. Rhoda and Carla were both in their thirties and had worked at McCormick since they left high school. Having weathered a lot of Mr. McCormick's temper tantrums, they often seemed to be utterly unaware of him and his anger—were even able to shout back at him. Aleta and Maggie had started at McCormick only two years before—and although Maggie had quickly developed the courage to yell back at him and the confidence to ignore him, Aleta still cowered at the sound of his voice.

"The invoices!" McCormick shrieked. And Aleta was certain she saw him stomp his foot just like a kid. "You remember invoices—without them being paid, I wouldn't be able to pay your salary."

"No, I'm sorry, I haven't finished them, Mr. McCormick," Aleta said, her face flushed with embarrassment. She looked down at her desk, at the incomplete tallies and slips of adding-machine tape. She had called the warehouse the day before and the foreman said he didn't have the necessary inventory figures.

It was the truth, but why didn't she have the nerve to tell Mr. McCormick? It wasn't just to protect the foreman, although certainly, if she told her boss that the foreman didn't have the figures, Mr. McCormick would simply direct his tantrum to the hapless factory head.

"I'm sorry," she repeated, her shoulders slumping. "I'm sorry. I'll get the figures done as quickly as possible."

In a moment as dramatic as any seen on the world's finest stages, the portly man sighed heavily and walked away.

"I suppose it's a little hard for the man who gives you your weekly check to compete with a glamorous prince," he muttered loudly. He whirled around at the door. "I want those invoices completed by one o'clock, Princess."

The women in the office waited as his heavy footsteps echoed from down the hall. They listened silently for the sound of Mr. McCormick's office door slamming before they released a collective, exaggerated giggle of relief.

"You really have to learn to stand up for yourself," Rhoda said. "You know, whenever he yells at me I just dish it right back at him. Last week, I put him in his place when he shouted about those payroll deduction sheets and he was so cowed, I got him to give me this coming Thursday afternoon off to go to my Billy's school play."

"I never let him get away with being abusive," Carla added. "Every time he flies off the handle, I tell him that it's unacceptable. He's a lot less personal in his attacks on me."

"But I never know what to say," Aleta said. "I get so . . . nervous that the words can't come out. I get all frozen inside."

"Just learn to fight back," Rhoda advised. "That doesn't mean that you have to yell as loudly as he does.

It just means you have to decide what limits you have. You're never going to survive if you can't fight back. You know, he's really a teddy bear if you turn around and show him you won't take any grief from him."

The women lapsed into silence. Aleta contemplated the work in front of her. It wasn't her fault that the monthly figures weren't ready, but why, oh why, didn't she have the guts to point that out?

"I guess this means you're not going with us to Marshall Field's," Maggie said. For weeks, the four office mates had planned a lunchtime trip to the downtown department store for its annual spring sale.

"It's just as well," Aleta shrugged. She had looked forward to the pleasant companionship more than the discounts, but it didn't matter now that Mr. McCormick was on the warpath. "I don't have any money left in my checking account anyway."

With a sympathetic nod, Maggie turned her attention back to her work.

Aleta allowed herself one last moment of fantasy, one last moment in the arms of Prince Giancarlo, one last moment when her lack of control over her life didn't press upon her, before she once more did battle with the pile of invoices, receipts, orders and checks.

One last moment in the arms of her prince.

At twelve-forty-five, she was alone at her desk—and still working at reconciling the monthly finances of the McCormick Company with the tally that the foreman had finally produced. Maggie had promised to bring back a sandwich for her, and the work she had accomplished after her office mates ran off with their cheery goodbyes made her think she just might make her one o'clock deadline.

Even if the warehouse had been late with the final figures.

Would Mr. McCormick ever change? she wondered.

He could be reasonable, even nice in a gruff sort of way. Aleta remembered the blizzardy afternoon in winter when he had closed the office early. Seeing the long lines at the bus stop outside his office window, he had driven each of the office mates and the receptionist to their homes. It had been an hours-long struggle against snarled traffic, six-foot drifts and blinding flakes—yet he had never complained and had led them in endless rounds of Christmas carols.

Sometimes Aleta wondered if the problem was her or him. Why was it so possible for her three office mates to survive his tirades with good humor and a shrug, while she could brood for days?

Was it because she couldn't fight for what she believed in? Wouldn't defend herself when she was wrongly accused?

Sometimes, she thought the fight had gone out of her when her mother had died five years before.

As she had sorted through the bills to be paid after the funeral, Aleta had suddenly realized the difficult sacrifices that her mother had made in order to give her a carefree adolescence. The problem was, when she was scrimping and saving, Mrs. Clayton hadn't prepared Aleta for the real world.

A real world of grumpy bosses and bill-paying and hard choices that left Aleta feeling increasingly trapped.

A real world in which every woman has to fight for herself.

In some ways, the change from happy-go-lucky teen to dull, mousy adult had been too extreme—few of Aleta's high school classmates would have recognized the somberly dressed, no-nonsense woman busily tallying McCormick's monthly invoices.

"You were made to be a princess," her mother had told her. Even now, Aleta affectionately laughed at the memory of her mother's loving whimsy. Probably because she was so intent on making her daughter feel as worthy as royalty to all of life's challenges, her mother had often told her that she was a direct descendant of one of the five Monticello families of distinction. And that she had been banished from Monticello after marrying an American—an American who had died of cancer when Aleta was only two.

A funny sort of delusion, but one that must have protected her from the grinding reality of being a single mom.

Some princess, Aleta muttered, clearing the memory on her calculator once more to add an exhaustive row of numbers. She had first heard her mother's story when she was nine years old and, on a shopping trip at the local grocery store, saw at the checkout counter a tabloid with a cover photo of the then-twenty-year-old prince.

"There's your husband-to-be," her mother had teased. And, in a lighthearted, seemingly casual manner, Mrs. Clayton had revealed her origins to her astonished daughter.

And yet Aleta could remember a wistful quality to her mother's words.

Nothing but love for her daughter could account for her mother's grand notions—her mother was dead now, but Aleta could hardly blame her for trying to inject some glamour, something special, into their lives.

The telephone rang, interrupting daydreaming and bill-figuring at once.

"There's a guy here to see you," the receptionist whined into the phone. "Should I send him back?"

Aleta stared at the phone. It was almost certainly another McCormick customer coming to plead his case—offering another worn excuse why his company couldn't pay their bill.

McCormick's going to love this, Aleta thought, reaching for the aspirin bottle in her middle drawer.

Still, she couldn't refuse to see the small business owner who had made the effort to talk to her in person. After all, so many people simply avoided her monthly calls to ask after McCormick's payment. She was, if she admitted the truth to herself, not very good at fighting with McCormick's customers who were late with their payments.

Mr. McCormick admitted this truth about her all the time.

"All right. Send him back here," Aleta agreed reluctantly.

What a terrible day, she thought, as she washed down two aspirin with a gulp of diet cola. Aleta hoped her visitor didn't take too much of her time so that she could finish April's invoices before Mr. McCormick checked on her again.

Chiding herself for being uncharitable, Aleta put on her best smile when her visitor walked into the office.

She didn't recognize him—a short, formally dressed man who looked as though he would be more at home in a ballroom than in the bookkeeping department of the McCormick Industrial Supply Company. An array of blue, gold and red ribbons and medals adorned his white, crisply starched jacket. He bowed slightly as he approached her desk and, as Aleta held out her hand to shake his, he bent down to kiss the air above her wrist.

He must owe us a lot of money, Aleta thought, as she racked her brain to think of who he might be.

"Are you Aleta Maria Coronado Clayton?" he asked, with a heavily accented voice. Aleta guessed that Spanish was his primary language. With some of the McCormick customers, she spoke the Spanish that her mother had taught her, but Aleta wondered if she would offend this stranger if she reverted to that language now.

"Yes, I am," Aleta said warily. How did this guy know her whole name? After all, the reminder notices she sent out on overdue bills were only signed with her first name—a cheery note, as if from a friend who simply wanted her money. A note which was followed, in two weeks, with a phone call during which she tried to be a little more insistent. Her last name was used with true deadbeats, but her middle names—well, never.

Something was very odd about this man.

And another thing, Aleta thought, as she leaned over her desk to get a second look—his fingernails were impeccably neat and his hands pale and clean. Most of the customers who came into her office came directly from their shops and factories. Their hands were dirty and their fingernails were worse.

"By the way, who are you?"

He bowed again.

"I am Captain Hortensio Manilla Coronado de Gustavio," he said, rising from his bow to his full height of, Aleta guessed, four feet eleven inches. "At your service. By a happy coincidence, I am your tenth cousin sixteen times removed. We are both descendants of Gustavio Coronado, who risked his life to save our beloved sovereign in the final battle of Monticello in 1456. You, of course, more directly than I."

Aleta decided it was time to get to the heart of the matter.

"Do you owe us money?"

Captain Whatever-his-name-was burst into laughter.

"I do not," he announced. "I am here to speak to you as a woman." He paused as she put her pencil down and stared at him. "You are, after all, the daughter of Anna Maria Aleta Gabriella Coronado who married one American named Barry Clayton." He paused at the effort of naming her father. "You are this Aleta, are you not?"

Aleta nodded slowly—her thoughts were coming together like tiny pieces of an intricate jigsaw puzzle. Her mother's oddly cadenced Spanish, an accent that she had explained was the Monticellan influence. Her mother telling her again and again, "If you are ever called into service to Monticello, you must do your duty." This captain's heavy accent, which matched her mother's.

His formality.

His clean and polished fingernails.

Those odd medals and ribbons on his jacket.

"Are you really from Monticello?" she asked, firmly putting her hands palm-down on the desk to stop the trembling within her. The question was not so much a query as an affirmation.

He nodded.

"I must call you into service to your mother's country," he said quietly. "I hope that you may find it within you to respond."

Aleta slumped backward into her chair. Nothing in all her days had ever shocked her so much as this tiny man and his not-so-tiny announcement.

"Spying?" She whispered, knowing in an instant that the prospect of leaving McCormick, or even Chicago, for a life of risk wasn't such a bad one.

He shook his head.

"Adventure?"

Her head was swimming with thoughts of exotic locales, daring endeavors, exciting...

He shrugged as if to suggest that what he had in mind might, just might, contain adventure.

"Tourism?" She faltered, remembering Monticello's most important industry. If there wasn't much intrigue, perhaps just a visit to the country would be great—if she could persuade Mr. McCormick to let her use her vacation time.

Again the shrug.

"Banking?" Knowing that she knew nothing, absolutely nothing, about the intricate Monticellan finance laws that made it an even safer haven than Switzerland to investors from all over the word.

He shook his head, to her relief.

Banking didn't sound that exciting.

"What do you have in mind?" she asked. "I mean, how can I be of service to Monticello?"

"Dinner," he announced with a slight bow.

Aleta opened her mouth, unable to speak.

This was certainly the craziest way for a man to ask a woman for a date!

Seeing her reaction, he reached for her diet cola can and motioned her to take a sip.

Aleta accepted the drink and gulped at the cool liquid. After a few deep breaths, she looked back up at the captain.

He seemed nice enough, but there weren't any bells ringing when she stared at him.

"With you?" If he was a tenth cousin sixteen times removed, she should go, if only to be hospitable. But the idea of dating a man who barely reached the top of her desk . . .

"With His Majesty, Prince Giancarlo, of course," Hortensio said, bowing at the mention of his sovereign's name.

"If I were a princess," Maggie mused, reaching her hand into the Frango mint box on her desk. "I would sleep until noon every day."

"If I were a princess," Carla said. "I would have all my clothes made by Chanel. And someone else would have to take care of my kids when I was tired."

"If I were a princess, I'd spend every day at the beach," Rhoda said, looking up briefly from her concentration on filing her nails. "And I'd quit this job in an instant and give Mr. McCormick a piece of my mind before I left."

The other two women nodded in agreement with her fantasy. They had gathered around Maggie's desk— eating a celebratory box of chocolates and abandoning all pretense of working.

After all, McCormick was out of the office for the afternoon!

And Aleta was going to be a princess!

Well, maybe it was just dinner, and probably it was with a bunch of other strangers who were chosen because of their relation to Monticello—although the Captain Hortensio de Whatever-his-name-was wasn't very specific on that last point. But three of the four bookkeepers for the McCormick Industrial Supply Company didn't doubt for a minute that Aleta would capture Prince Giancarlo's eye, his heart and the throne.

And the fourth bookkeeper—the possible future princess—wasn't talking.

Aleta sat at her desk, drumming her fingers against the steel top, staring into space—or rather, staring at the bulletin board upon which the McCormick orders for the coming month were tacked.

But she wasn't studying the orders.

She wasn't even aware of them. She was too busy remembering her visitor and the reason for his visit.

Shaking with excitement had been her first response, followed by immediate suspicion of the captain. But, after giving him a quick quiz on Monticello history— most of it Aleta had gotten from her mother or from the *International Snoop*—the captain seemed to be the real article, a real Monticello native, and quite possibly even the aide-de-camp to the prince, as he claimed to be.

An invitation he had proffered, with her name engraved in gold leaf, had clinched the deal.

She said yes.

After he left, with instructions to meet at the Pump Room, only Chicago's toniest restaurant, Aleta had leapt about the office with delight. Delight was followed by nerves—after all, it wasn't every day an ordinary bookkeeper went to a party with a bona fide prince.

Even if it was probably in a dining room crowded with other descendants of the Monticellan conquistador Gustavio Coronado, even if she only saw the prince from a distance, even if she felt nervous and gawky and out of place.

To see the man she had dreamed of, in increasingly mature terms, since that moment at the grocery store checkout line when her mother had called him her husband-to-be.

Then she was stopped short by fear.

What if she did something stupid, something unprotocol? What if she spilled her drink? What if she tripped and fell? What if no one at the party talked to her? She didn't even know how to curtsy, and she wasn't sure if Americans were supposed to.

When her other office mates returned with their bulging shopping bags, she told them her news. They were as giddy with excitement as she and, unable to sit down, Aleta had frantically paced. She walked back and forth across the ten feet of the office so many times that Maggie told her that she was sure to wear down the carpet.

The office mates wanted to know every detail, every smidgen of the conversation, every nuance of the captain's appearance. Then, they pulled Aleta's *International Snoop* from her bag and pored over the photos of the prince and the lurid descriptions of his escapades. They fingered the engraved invitation until Aleta had taken it back...after all, it would serve as her only souvenir of the evening.

"You know, these royal marriages never turn out well," Rhoda said. "After all, these princes have been raised from babies to act as if they were...well, you know, princes!"

"Yeah, they never help out with the kids," Carla chimed in.

"That's what servants are for," Maggie corrected. "Do you think princesses have to sort laundry or vacuum the royal ballroom?"

"No, but Carla's got a point," Rhoda said. "Plenty of princesses have had to take care of a sick heir to the throne while the daddy prince is off playing polo or taking cruises in the Pacific with bimbo duchesses. It'd be like being a single mom."

"A very rich single mom," Maggie added.

Exhausted by the war of nerves within herself, Aleta lapsed into a slouch at her desk—staring mindlessly at the hapless stack of papers that she had abandoned all hope of working through today. Thank God Mr. McCormick had left the office for the day without even remembering the one o'clock deadline he had given her.

"But if I had to be a princess, I would eat nothing but caviar and champagne," Carla said dreamily. "And never again would polyester touch my skin—it would be silks and satins forever after."

"If I were a princess and my prince didn't act right, I would take a lover," Rhoda announced.

Maggie and Carla giggled.

"They don't let you take a lover," Carla said. "It's like being a nun—after you produce your heir and a spare, you're consigned to no sex—unless His Royal Highness comes through."

She looked significantly at Aleta, who turned scarlet. Discussions of a more...intimate nature had always embarrassed Aleta and her office mates often teased her about her shyness about sex. But suddenly Carla's words fell flat in a way that the lighthearted, good-natured teasing of the past had not.

The stakes were suddenly high as Aleta's friends realized that she was taking her upcoming dinner very seriously.

"Hey, what are you going to wear tonight?" Maggie asked, abruptly shifting the conversation to prevent further embarrassment for her friend. "The Pump Room is absolutely the most fancy place you can go. There's no way you can wear what you've got on now."

Aleta looked down at her plain black skirt and white blouse, the latter with a small, but very visible, ink stain on its left sleeve. Maggie was right—an outfit that was serviceable for the office wasn't the sort of thing one wore to a meeting with a prince.

"Do you have something special that you can change into?" Rhoda asked.

Deflated, Aleta considered her wardrobe—it was easy to visualize her closet, since it was nearly empty. Jeans, sweatpants and T-shirts for weekends. Plain skirts for work to be paired with ladylike blouses and sweaters.

She shook her head.

"I don't have anything better than this."

"You don't go on enough dates, because if you did, you'd be out shopping every day like Maggie is," Carla teased. "And you'd have a closet full of clothes to show for it."

All four women laughed and Carla and Rhoda both decided that they had to share the news of Aleta's invitation with a few friends, family members and heaven knew who else. Within seconds, the two older women were on the phone, whispering their excited comments and embellishments to Aleta's story.

But Maggie didn't need to phone anyone—she stared hard at Aleta. She knew that Aleta didn't date much— just the infrequent blind dates that Maggie set up. She believed it had to do with Aleta's mother's death, which seemed to have irrevocably changed Aleta from a light-hearted young woman into an older, more sober one.

Mrs. Clayton's death had simply knocked the wind out of her friend.

What a poor little princess, Maggie thought.

Without noticing it, Maggie had slipped into the assumption that Aleta was poised on the brink of a royal romance.

"I have an idea," Maggie said brightly. "How about if we cut out of the office early and run over to my apartment? You can pick out any dress you like. I even have my old prom dress—it would be perfect on you."

Aleta brightened considerably. Five years before, she had thought it the most unbelievably glamorous dress she had ever seen. She could almost feel herself transported back to Maggie's bedroom—back to the afternoon she had watched her best friend dress for a prom that Aleta couldn't afford to attend, that Aleta didn't have the heart to attend.

At the time, she had been filled with immature regret and rage at the injustice of her mother's recent death.

But now she remembered only how much she had thought that Maggie looked like a princess.

Just like a princess.

"Oh, Maggie, would you really let me borrow it?"

Maggie's heart nearly broke at her friend's simple enthusiasm. If it had been any other girl but Aleta going to dinner at the Pump Room, Maggie would have been jealous enough to scratch her eyes out—figuratively, of course. But, Maggie remembered the carefree girl Aleta had been in high school, and she had witnessed the radical changes brought on by Mrs. Clayton's sudden, tragic death.

There wasn't any other girl in the world who deserved this more than Aleta, Maggie resolved, thinking of her own lilac prom dress and how wonderful it would look on Aleta at the Pump Room.

And maybe in a picture in the *International Snoop* with a suitable caption.

Miss Aleta Clayton, wearing Miss Maggie O'Hara's prom dress, shares a glass of champagne with Prince Giancarlo of Monticello.

"But, you're sure that the prom dress would be all right for the Pump Room?" Aleta asked tentatively.

"Oh, it'll be perfect," Maggie counseled, with a confidence that she didn't quite feel. After all, she had never been to the swank restaurant where the upper crust of Chicago society and visiting VIPs met. But why should she let her ignorance stand in the way of giving good advice? Especially when Aleta looked like she needed every ounce of confidence she could borrow. "Come on, grab your purse, let's go. McCormick's not coming back 'til tomorrow. It's the first day of the golf season for him."

Aleta picked up her bag and turned off her adding machine.

"What if the prince turns out to be a jerk in person?" Carla asked, putting down her phone. "I mean, there are plenty of women who have married a prince only to find out he's a frog."

"She should still marry him," Maggie said brightly. "Not all marriages between commoners and royalty turn out poorly. Look at..." She faltered. "Well, it doesn't matter. If she marries him, she'll never have to worry about Mr. McCormick again. Or any other mundane problem."

"Assuming she actually gets a chance to talk to the prince," Rhoda cautioned, holding her hand against the receiver of her phone. "Remember, he's a playboy—no offense, Aleta, but he'll probably have half a dozen bimbos hanging on him tonight. Remember, he's grown up all his life hearing about how every woman would kill to have a chance at him. With a man like that, you'd have to do the chasing. And it's a toss-up whether he'd be worth it.''

"Yeah, Aleta, darling, you have to think seriously about this," Carla protested. "If you marry him just because he's a prince, you might not realize what kind of person he is inside. Other girls have made that mistake," she added significantly.

Throughout the afternoon, Aleta had pretty much been able to ignore her friends' comments, the ones that had suggested that Prince Giancarlo was less a prince and more a frog. But Rhoda and Carla were getting very close to the most intimate secret she kept within herself.

A secret so special that even Maggie didn't know.

Aleta knew she was already in love.

"You're wrong about all this," Aleta said solemnly. "I think he's wonderful."

"But you've never met him and you don't have much in common," Rhoda pointed out. "You don't know how to ski, and that seems to be his biggest hobby. You hate loud music and he's in nightclubs every night. You don't know that much about him and what you do know doesn't sound very good. The *Snoop* says, and I quote, 'he's spoiled, petulant, demanding, aloof...'"

"I know everything about him," Aleta interrupted. "I know what kind of food he likes—foie gras and braised pheasant. I know the names of his former girlfriends—the Contessa de Larimar was his most recent. I know his favorite color—purple. I know everything about the man and I love him."

At those last three potent words, an uncomfortable silence came over the room. Aleta slapped her hand over her mouth, but the words—her most precious secret—had already been said.

Carla wiped her chocolate-covered fingers. Rhoda told the person at the other end of her line that she would call back, slid her chair back to her own desk, put her nail file back in her top drawer and studied the month's payroll sheets.

Aleta stood at her desk, purse in hand, suddenly realizing how very terrifying it was when a very special, very private secret wasn't a secret anymore.

I love him.

She had said it aloud.

"Oh, come on, girl!" Maggie tugged enthusiastically at her sleeve and the mood of the room instantly brightened. "We've got to get that prom dress out of my closet. It'll look perfect on you. Maybe we still have time to hang it up in the bathroom while we run the shower—you know, to get the wrinkles out."

As she was pulled from the office, Aleta looked one last time at Maggie's desk. The prince's pictures were spread out under discarded chocolate mint wrappings. He smiled up at her, at every *Snoop* reader.

But his smile seemed haunted, and it was as if Aleta noticed for the first time that he might not be the carefree, fun-loving man she—and the world—thought he was.

Aleta shivered.

A fairy tale was coming true and she didn't want it to be ruined by reality.

Chapter Two

I could just kill Maggie.

Or maybe myself, Aleta thought, nervously twisting a section of the satin which cascaded from her waist. Standing at the entranceway to the Pump Room, observing for the first time the elegant restaurant within the Ambassador East Hotel, Aleta knew she had made a terrible mistake.

And, in her heart of hearts, she knew that it was unfair to blame Maggie—after all, her friend meant well. And she herself had been the one who had thought the dress was a confection of dreams when Maggie had worn it for the prom.

Now it seemed a wilted reminder of how inadequate she felt in the face of the glamorous restaurant.

Aleta wasn't the sort of woman who ordinarily worried about clothes. A simple skirt, a neutral jacket, a plain blouse—those were the sorts of choices she made every weekday morning. For evening, when she re-

laxed at home after work, a pair of jeans was more her
style than an evening gown—especially since it had been
months since she had gone on a date.

She knew that clothes weren't the most important
thing a woman had to think about.

But Aleta also knew that, for tonight, the right
clothes were important.

And the dress Maggie had loaned her was wrong.

Very wrong.

Looking into the dining room at the smartly dressed
women—with their short, swingy skirts and their bright
jackets—Aleta's stomach had done a half gainer. These
women belonged in the Pump Room—they held their
glasses of champagne with confidence and negotiated
with ease the intricate place settings of at least three
forks and an equal number of spoons and knives. These
women who peppered the dining room otherwise pop-
ulated with men in dark, respectable suits—none of
them would have worn a lilac prom gown to the Pump
Room.

With matching lilac shoes.

And matching lilac bag and gloves.

And a stiff, voluminous skirt that took up the entire
width of the dark hallway leading into the dining room.
A hallway peppered with hundreds, maybe thousands,
of photos of the celebrities who dined here.

Stars, politicians, writers, athletes.

Not a bookkeeper among them, Aleta was willing to
bet.

And not a lilac gown to be seen.

Thank God she couldn't see Captain Hortensio
Whatever-his-name-was or the prince, or she would
have instantly prayed for the floor of the restaurant to
part and swallow her up.

I must look like a graduating senior who's lost her high school, Aleta thought grimly.

She pulled off the lilac elbow-length gloves that had seemed so glamorous when Maggie had shoved them at her.

"Is there something I can do for you?"

Aleta looked up at the maitre d', whose tentative question and piercing stare suggested that even he thought she was out of place.

Aleta swallowed. Hard.

"No, I don't think so." She choked the words out.

Unable to maintain her composure any longer, she turned and rushed down the dark hall that led back to the lobby of the hotel. A quick glance at her watch confirmed that, with only five minutes before six, she didn't have time to go home and change into something a little less...attention grabbing. But she at least had time to find a bathroom and scrub off the ridiculously heavy makeup which Maggie had insisted on applying to her face. And maybe untease her hair. And take off the heavy false eyelashes that Maggie had put on her. And the sparkling rhinestone earrings.

And maybe just cry a million tears because this was her one chance to break out of being just an ordinary bookkeeper, if only for one night and the whole evening was ruined because...

She was churning with all of these thoughts, around and around in an increasingly frenetic circle, when she ran headlong into a large tweed-covered chest.

A tweed-covered chest connected to two very strong hands that gripped her arms, holding her up as she was very nearly about to trip on the dark, plush carpet.

She looked up, her breath knocked out of her, shocked by force of the collision.

Straight into the eyes of the prince.

There was no mistaking him.

Even if he wasn't two-dimensional on a glossy 8 ½ x 11 inch magazine cover with an address label on his chest.

Their eyes connected, and, for Aleta, the rest of the world dissolved. She wasn't a bookkeeper, she wasn't behind on putting together the month's invoices for McCormick, she wasn't self-conscious about Maggie's outfit. She was suddenly in the arms of the man she had worshiped since she was a child. She felt the pressure of his hands against her arms and she swore she would feel that imprint forever.

He was the prince, a man she had met so many times before—in check-out counter tabloids, society pages and unauthorized biographies. He was a man who she believed she knew—who she was certain she knew more intimately than any other man.

And yet, there were surprises to the reality of him. Surprises which made her shiver with delight.

His eyes were much bluer than she expected—an intensity that wasn't communicated in pictures that were so often shot as he defensively held an arm against the inquiring lens of the photographer. He was also taller, more substantial than she expected, although that was difficult to believe since his photos were nearly always the wide-angle shots that made him seem like a giant. His hair was black, she had expected that much, but surprisingly deeply hued—the thick, tousled curls looked almost like jet.

But the biggest surprise was how relaxed he seemed, his face momentarily free of the arrogant, bad-boy scowl so often caught by the frantic press.

At least he could afford to be relaxed.

He wasn't dressed in a ridiculous prom outfit, simply a subdued, tweed suit that made Maggie's prom gown look even more out of place.

If that was possible.

He let go of Aleta long enough to reach down to pick up the ghastly lilac puddle of gloves and bag that now lay at her feet.

"*Señora,* you dropped these...." he said with only the faintest Spanish accent. His stare softened to one of pity as he pressed Maggie's wilted accessories into her hands. "Is there something wrong?"

Aleta's eyes widened in panic.

"No," she said, her voice sounding strangely distant. "It's just..."

She pointed behind her, to the swank restaurant, as if it were a den of evil.

"I'm overdressed."

He nodded but said nothing and was about to move on when she clutched at his arm. His eyes instantly narrowed with concern and suspicion, changing hue from baby blue to the color of a deep and restless sea. She felt his muscles tightening beneath his jacket and, though he continued to smile, his tension was evident.

He was ready.

And wary.

Prepared for anything.

Aleta, you idiot! she thought.

He probably thinks you're some sort of crazy lunatic or a fan or, worse, a member of the press. The poor guy gets followed by every fortune-hunting woman and tabloid writer on either side of the Atlantic.

"I'm Aleta Clayton," she explained, hoping that a simple introduction would bridge the gulf between them.

Her name didn't ring any bells with him.

He continued to smile distantly, without the softening of his features reaching his eyes. It was a smile designed to carry a celebrated prince through a grueling day of public appearances. Obviously this dinner was going to have a hundred guests—and the name Aleta Clayton certainly didn't mean anything.

There was no reason it should.

She wondered at the differences between them.

For her, the evening was to have been a fairy tale vacation from the ordinariness of her life.

For him, it was probably another in a long string of perfectly forgettable public appearances.

Aleta tried again.

"I'm supposed to have dinner with you and…the rest of the people who were invited," she added lamely, reluctantly letting her arm drop to her side. "Captain Hortensio Something-or-other told me to meet him here."

She could crawl into the earth after the way he looked her up and down, seeming to study with disbelief the woman before him. Disbelief tinged with horror—as if Aleta were some embodiment of a nightmare. His blue eyes clouded over and he held himself apart from her, studying her.

Without meaning to, Aleta felt her chin lift with defiance. She might be a commoner. She might be a bookkeeper, an ordinary working girl. She might be an American. And she might be dressed in a most ridiculous lilac outfit—but Aleta had every right to be here, in Chicago, in the Pump Room, in his arms.

Well, maybe not in his arms.

How could she be thinking of an embrace when he clearly couldn't stand the sight of her?

"You're Aleta Maria Coronado Clayton?" he asked, with a disbelief that grew as he regarded her outrageous costume.

"You're really good at memorizing guest lists," Aleta blurted, impressed that he knew her whole name. How many other names did a prince have to keep track of on a typical day?

"I suppose I am," he conceded.

"Your Majesty, I mean, Your Highness—" She paused. What did one call a prince—especially one who looked like he deserved his reputation for being cold and aloof? Aleta struggled to put her feelings into words. "I can't possibly go in there because, you see, I thought this was a fancy restaurant...I mean it *is* a fancy restaurant, but I didn't realize that nobody, nobody would be dressed up like this. I thought that everyone would..."

Stop babbling! Aleta commanded herself, but it was difficult to get her mouth to obey when Giancarlo stared at her with an utterly cold, expressionless face.

It was also hard to stop talking when she was trying to drown out the voice in her head that was insisting that maybe, just maybe, the *International Snoop* was right—maybe Prince Giancarlo wasn't very nice. Maybe he was a little aloof. Maybe a little cold. Maybe a little arrogant and disdainful of the people around him.

Because any other man, any other commoner, would have stopped her—with a smile, with an interruption, with a comment. Anything, anything...if only to put her out of her misery.

Not just a blank stare.

"I didn't realize people wouldn't be dressed up like...this," she finished lamely, looking down at the wrinkled satin that had seemed so completely dazzling when she had twirled in front of the full-length mirror in Maggie's studio apartment.

He studied her for a moment, and Aleta felt herself becoming even more self-conscious. Coming to some sort of decision, his arm shot out and he took her elbow, turning her away from the restaurant.

"Accompany me to the lobby," he said.

Aleta gaped at him as they walked. She resented his forcefulness, his presumption, his command—he was acting as if he was some sort of . . . prince.

And yet, he was the man she loved, wasn't he?

They stopped at the doorway leading into the lobby.

"I believe that you have been crying and might want to freshen up in the ladies' room."

Aleta touched her cheek and felt the damp evidence of tears.

"I shall return and meet you at that couch."

The prince pointed to a French Provincial love seat in a discreet corner of the lobby. He slipped his arm from hers and disappeared into a waiting elevator. In an instant, the doors closed behind him.

Aleta stared after him, wondering at their encounter. Then she became uncomfortably aware of the curious stares of people standing in the lobby. Were they staring at her because she had been talking to the prince, or because of Maggie's dress?

She wanted to run and hide—just grab up her balloonlike skirt and run as quickly as her matching pumps could carry her.

A single conversation with the prince and I blew it, she thought dismally. *I could have talked about Monticello, about my mother's dream of returning there someday, or about his trip to Chicago.*

I could have talked about the weather, if nothing else! she berated herself. *Instead, what did I talk about?*

Maggie's dress.

The covert stares of onlookers galvanized her to action. Aleta wasn't used to this much attention and she didn't like it. Not one bit.

Just act as a princess would act, she thought, remembering the prince and his cool calm.

She raised her chin and threw back her shoulders into regal posture. She lifted a delicate handful of fabric from the skirt of the gown and marched serenely to the ladies' room.

Studiously ignoring the people whose heads swiveled to keep up with her.

This acting royal is hard work, she thought as she locked the private ladies' room door behind her. Her shoulders relaxed and she looked into the mirror. Without meaning to, she smiled at the disaster.

No doubt about it, she looked absolutely ridiculous. Light brown hair piled way too high, makeup streaked with tears and one of Maggie's false eyelashes beginning to disengage itself at the outer corner of her eye.

"My evening with the prince," she told the mirror. "One thirty-second conversation to tell my future grandkids about—they'll probably roll their eyes and think Grandma's crazy."

With a start, she realized she wasn't even thinking of the dress, the embarrassment, the lashes. Or grandkids.

She was thinking of him.

He was even more handsome in person than he was in print—and Aleta had seen an awful lot of pictures of the prince over the years since she had begun buying any magazine that had an article about him.

"I'm going to have to join a convent after he goes back to Monticello," she said, yanking off one eyelash.

Any other man—the sort of man who would ever want to marry her, the sort of man she would meet after this evening was over—wouldn't stack up against Him, would always be measured against the memory of this evening's brief embrace.

When he had steadied her in his arms. When he had kept her from falling.

Yet the very fact she could joke with herself about him was a measure of how much she could let go of her infatuation. After all, he would be remembered for a scant moment in the hallway leading from the Pump Room to the hotel lobby.

Fortunately for her real-life future, he had confirmed every snide *International Snoop* report about his aloofness, his arrogance, his coolness. Why, he had actually commanded her to follow him into the lobby while he made his getaway, hadn't he?

Resolving to not think of the future, she pulled the twenty or so bobby pins from her hair, washed the lash adhesive from her eyelids and took off the rhinestone drop earrings. In only a few minutes, she had pulled her light brown hair into a relaxed chignon and her sole makeup was a light dusting of powder and a pale peach lipstick that made her eyes seem even larger. She felt more comfortable without all the extra sparkle.

Somehow, she confessed to herself, she looked better without it.

There was nothing she could do about the dress, but she stuffed the gloves into her bag. Then she got an idea. She reached beneath her skirt, pulled off the stiff, crinoline half-slip and stuffed it into the wastebasket.

"That's a lot better," she said, only now aware of how the crinoline had made her legs feel itchy. What a relief to be comfortable again.

I'll buy you another dress, she mentally promised Maggie, although she had no idea with what money.

She then smoothed down her skirt and, as she studied herself in the mirror, was surprised at the difference.

I almost look pretty, she thought with amazement. Although it had been so long since she had regarded the mirror with anything other than a glance to ensure she wasn't walking out of the house in utter disarray that she wasn't a judge of whether she was pretty this evening or pretty always.

She took a deep, relaxing breath and pulled her shoulders up into perfect posture.

Just pretend you're a princess, she thought to herself, dreading the walk across the lobby. She wanted to go home. After all, there was no way that the prince was going to spend another second with her. His attention would be focused on the other guests—dignitaries and local celebrities, no doubt. A sweat suit, a pint of double chocolate-chip ice cream and the movie of the week sounded awfully inviting.

But she knew she should stay. There would be no honor in explaining to Maggie, Rhoda, Carla—even future grandchildren—that she had chickened out.

It would be so much in character for her, she admitted to herself. She never fought against Mr. McCormick when he railed against her work and she never fought against the nerves she felt when faced by new and strange tasks.

Like dates.

Maggie had stopped setting her up on blind dates because she kept putting off the actual meetings with prospective suitors, until, at last, they would often give up.

Running home and hiding in her studio apartment was exactly what Aleta was most likely to do.

You coward, she thought, staring bleakly at her reflection.

But the overhead light captured the Monticellan pendant at her neck—a momentary sparkle of gold rendition of the battle of 1456 galvanized her.

Why was she always so afraid to stand up to others?

Why was she always so afraid to fight for what she wanted?

Why was she always so afraid to take the pleasures that life offered—even a life as ordinary as her own?

No, Aleta Maria Coronado Clayton was made of tougher stuff, she thought, pulling her shoulders back.

Just for tonight, just for the few hours that she would be at the Pump Room, she wanted to claim happiness to last a lifetime. A once-in-a-lifetime moment to meet her prince and she wasn't willing to let it turn into another failure, another instance of her lack of gumption.

In the lobby, she attracted as much attention as before, but somehow the stares were more respectful and, in the case of several men, tinged with that special appraisal that gives a woman confidence. Aleta barely noticed these stares—desperate to hang on to her courage, she was determined to look neither to her left or her right. Her head held high, she walked across the marble floor, nearly not noticing the French love seat.

And the prince.

She stopped in her tracks and almost dissolved into tears at the sight of him.

What a man, she thought. *He's just as wonderful-looking as I've always dreamed he was.*

He was dressed in the white uniform that Aleta recognized from state occasions reported in the *International Snoop,* complete with a brilliant purple sash that was covered with impressive medals and ribbons and gold braid.

There wasn't a woman alive who wouldn't fantasize about loosening the tidy black tie at his throat.

And Aleta certainly felt very alive at the moment.

As he rose from his seat, Aleta felt the busy lobby plummet into silence as onlookers dropped all pretense of engaging in any activity other than staring at the prince and at Aleta. Aleta felt her cheeks tingle with self-consciousness, but she kept her eyes studiously trained on the prince.

He took her hand in his and kissed the air above it.

She started to question him, to haltingly thank him for the obvious effort to make her feel comfortable by dressing as if this were the occasion and the place for formal attire. He had done this for her, to make her more comfortable, to give her confidence.

But with the barest frown, he silenced her.

"One should always dress for dinner," he said, pulling her arm into his.

"But you weren't going to dress like this!" she whispered as he led her into the restaurant. "You just dressed like this because I made such a fool of myself."

"One should always dress for dinner," he repeated firmly.

Though he had spoken in a crisp, somewhat abrasive tone, Aleta's gratitude and relief at someone dressed with her formality made her smile with delight. She didn't have the chance to thank him. A mob of reporters erupted from the revolving doors—shouting questions and snapping pictures. A shocking flash of light blinded her. She reflexively shrunk back from Giancarlo, though he held even more tightly to her hand. A piercing headache, a strike of lightning within the lobby, a bomb exploding...

"It's just the damned photographers," the prince whispered. "Smile brightly and don't look directly at them or you'll have trouble seeing."

Blinking against the afterimages left by the flashes, Aleta allowed herself to be led, nearly blind, into the dark hallway of the dining room. The stocky Captain Hortensio, dressed now in a subdued charcoal-gray suit, met them and stood behind them, blocking the three photographers who crowded against the door.

"Gentlemen, gentlemen, the prince is merely trying to have a private dinner," Aleta heard the captain explain. "He will be available for photos later this evening. This is a private dinner with a friend of the Monticello royal family."

"Who is she?"

"Is she a Chicagoan?"

"What about reports that the queen is pressuring Prince Giancarlo to marry?"

"Is this a royal match?"

Aleta thought she would die of embarrassment as the reporters shouted questions at them. She looked up at the prince, fearful that the questions about her had angered him.

To be caught in a photograph with her was probably not going to make him happy, either. After all, he was a man who had been linked with the most beautiful, glamorous, wealthy, titled women in the world. Indeed, his face was hardened with tension and she didn't have the nerve to say anything.

She didn't know whether to pity him, for the constant scrutiny and invasions of his privacy. To be angry with him, for his cold, commandeering manner. Or to love him, simply to love him.

To let this night be a wonderful memory.

And leave herself open for the heartache that accompanies every unrequited love.

The reporters' shouted questions only stopped when Hortensio loudly promised a press conference immediately after the dessert course.

At the mention of dessert and the promise of food, Aleta remembered that this was dinner—and that she hadn't eaten a thing, not a single bite of her lunchtime sandwich, from the moment she met Hortensio. She would have thought she was too nervous to eat, but now the prospect of a little nourishment excited her.

Certainly, the dinner offered to the guests of the Prince of Monticello had to be better than the TV dinners she had stacked in her freezer.

They approached the desk of the maitre d', who smiled broadly at the prince, rubbing his hands together with delight at the sight of his honored guest.

"Your Highness," he said and bowed from the waist. When he rose, his eyes flickered briefly over Aleta. If he recognized her as the woman he had questioned ten minutes before, he didn't show it. "Mademoiselle, right this way."

Aleta felt herself being propelled in the direction of the maitre d' by Giancarlo's strong arm on her elbow. She obediently followed the maitre d' through the dining room, aware of the deferential, wide-eyed stares of the other diners.

The maitre d' led them to a table at the rear of the dining room, behind an elegant lacquered Chinese screen. Aleta stared thoughtfully at the chair that the maitre d' had offered her at the table set for four.

"Is there something the matter?" Giancarlo asked.

Aleta shook her head.

"No, of course not," she answered and took her seat. Giancarlo sat opposite her and the maitre d' disappeared.

"I guess I thought that there would be lots of other people," she added. "You know, like maybe all the Chicagoans who have relatives in Monticello. There have to be more of them than just me."

Giancarlo smiled, a brief hint of friendliness which didn't reach his eyes. Since they had met in the lobby, his face had lapsed into the cold, haunted look that sometimes seemed part of his public persona.

"No, there will only be myself, Hortensio and one other Monticellan to entertain you," he said, pulling his napkin onto his lap. "I hope you aren't disappointed."

Baffled, yes. Disappointed...

"Not at all."

He looked up at her from behind his menu. His eyes were coolly appraising, as if he were trying to tally up her good and bad points in some objective fashion. It was clear he didn't want to be with her, and certainly, if being a prince meant you had to have dinner with a hundred different strangers in a hundred different cities, Aleta couldn't blame him.

Yet, why was he forced to have dinner with her?

She wasn't powerful, wasn't rich, wasn't anyone who could help his country. A published photo of the two of them dining this evening wouldn't publicize Monticello in any way.

Why was he here?

Who had ordered him to do this?

Who could order a prince?

She looked at him while he studied his menu with enormous concentration. She would have liked to ask him a dozen questions—but he didn't look as though he had any intention of answering them.

Or of speaking to her, if he could avoid it.

She thought of thanking him again for changing his clothes, so that their conversation could start on a good note.

But it had seemed so obvious that her initial thanks had made him uncomfortable.... And besides, why did she have to be eternally grateful for one admittedly very nice gesture when it was nestled in a series of cool actions which would be regarded as rude if committed by a commoner?

Let him make the first conversational move, Aleta resolved, picking up her napkin.

After all, wasn't there a protocol rule about not starting conversations with royalty until spoken to?

Having a funny feeling that royalty was going to look at his menu until he memorized it, Aleta decided to look at her own.

Might be nice to find out what was so engrossing about it!

They sat in silence for several minutes. Baked Brie *en croûte.* Breast of duck roasted in a bed of pine nuts and kumquats. Carpaccio with olive oil and capers.

She stared at the list of appetizers and hoped that he would say something.

From behind the elegant screen, Hortensio appeared. He brought with him a tall, gawky youth whose gray suit was ill fitting in every spot that on Hortensio was the smooth line of expensive tailoring. The two men bowed to Giancarlo, but the shrug the prince responded with suggested that the formality of royal protocol was often dispensed with.

Aleta put her menu on her plate, glad someone she knew she could talk to would be with them—even if it was a four-foot-eleven captain she had only met this afternoon.

"Miss Clayton," Hortensio bowed briefly in her direction. "May I present Rudolph, my assistant."

Rudolph smiled shyly at Aleta and took his seat. He immediately pulled from his inside pocket a notebook—but quickly returned it to its hiding place when Hortensio loudly and pointedly harrumphed.

"We will order a drink first," Giancarlo said and though he spoke with utter civility, Aleta was certain that there was an underlying note of hostility toward his two aides. His blue eyes maintained the cold, deep cloudiness that Aleta had noticed when she'd met him.

"Of course, Your Highness," Hortensio said. "I think it is perfectly acceptable to relax first and get to know one another before we begin."

"If we're going to relax first, what's going to happen second?" she blurted out, but before she could receive an answer, several waiters had descended on the foursome. A fluted glass was placed before her, and one of the staff solicitously unruffled her napkin and placed it on her lap. A sommelier popped open a bottle of what Aleta instantly recognized as one of the most expensive champagnes of France—the prince's favorite, according to the magazines. She looked up at him, but he didn't appear very happy about the wine.

In fact, he looked downright mad.

Hortensio raised his glass, a wide grin on his face.

"To our most beloved sovereign, Queen Marianya," he said. "To the continuation of the principality of Monticello, to the unbroken lineage of the royal family, to the four hundred years of freedom from Spanish tyranny, to the ancestors of the Coronado line, to..."

"That is sufficient," the prince said quietly.

Hortensio stopped and looked at the prince. At first, it looked as if the two men might exchange words. Angry words. Hortensio stared down the prince, refusing to falter, to look away from the steely eyes of his royal employer. Aleta wondered at the charged atmosphere that had developed—she almost wished that the unspoken argument that seemed to rage between the two silent men would explode, just so that she could understand it.

"Well, then I shall propose a more simple toast," Hortensio said dramatically. "To the royal family, which I have served since I took my first breath and for whose continuation I would sacrifice my life and the lives of my unborn children."

Boy, these guys sure know how to throw a fun party! Aleta thought, wondering how this prince would get any dates at all if he wasn't a prince. And wasn't wildly handsome. And wasn't very wealthy. And wasn't sexy enough to make her heart—and undoubtedly the hearts of every other woman he met—gallop like a Thoroughbred.

She took a sip of her champagne, allowing the dazzling bubbles to burst in her mouth like a thousand dying stars. The promise of this evening had been destroyed.

She had expected to be part of a cocktail party. She had expected to be nervous, to drink nearly flat champagne, to have her feet stepped on several times by people who wouldn't apologize, to eat greasy appetizers served by a waiter who carried a tray but who would have run out of napkins. She had expected to talk to people who would be as bored by her as she would be by them. She had expected to see the prince from a distance, perhaps close enough to see him smile, to overhear a word from his lips.

She had expected to go home to hear a message from Maggie on her answering machine and she had expected to spend the rest of the evening giving her friend every detail of the guests' clothes, hairdo, conversation—perhaps saving some smidgen of her impressions of the prince as a private, intimate secret between herself . . . and herself. She had expected an evening that would be a warm memory to carry within her, a moment to be savored long after Maggie and her other friends were gossiping about some other event in someone else's life.

But this evening, this evening of a shared dinner, was nothing less than a nightmare. The nightmare of discovering that her dream wasn't real.

Her dream of the prince, the man within the royal.

He didn't like being with her.

He didn't like her.

In all her fantasies, in all her daydreams, she had never accounted for this possibility.

The foursome sat quietly and Aleta wracked her brain for appropriate conversational starters for nobility. If the rules of protocol demanded that commoners not speak to royalty until spoken to, didn't that create a responsibility on the part of royalty to speak?

"Well, enough relaxing chitchat," Hortensio said, breaking the uncomfortable silence. "Perhaps a few questions to help us get to know one another?"

Aleta nodded tentatively. With discussion at a dead halt and Giancarlo's face turned to nothing short of a cold, hostile mask, she was ready for anything.

"So, Miss Clayton, have you ever been married before?" Hortensio asked, with a forced casual tone.

She shook her head quickly.

"Have you had any children?"

What a weird question to ask someone you hardly know! She looked at Giancarlo, who didn't look up from his study of the menu. Then she noticed Rudolph sliding his notebook from his jacket pocket.

Maybe her mother hadn't taught her enough about Monticellan customs. Maybe what seemed like stilted conversation and downright rudeness was simply the Monticello way of doing things.

Like studying a menu until you could probably recite the selections in your sleep, she thought grimly, or writing in notebooks at the dinner table.

"No, I haven't," she answered. Perhaps it was simply natural in Monticello to inquire about children first. "Do you have children?"

He waved away her question, and Aleta realized her mistake.

"Oh, yes, you mentioned you hadn't any children," she said.

The prince's head shot up from his menu.

"In Hortensio's toast," she explained. The scowl on the prince's face deepened and his jaw clenched with anger. "About how he's going to sacrifice them for the Monticello royal . . ."

The prince slammed shut the menu and reached for the wine list. Aleta swore she never met a man so intrigued by restaurant selections—or so determined to avoid talking to her. Rudolph began to scribble in his notebook, his pen scraping at the paper. Without looking up, the prince grabbed the tiny notebook and it disappeared behind the hefty leather wine list.

Hortensio harrumphed.

Rudolph folded his hands on his lap.

Aleta took another sip of her champagne.

"Have you ever been arrested or been a plaintiff or defendant in any civil or criminal lawsuit?" Hortensio asked.

Aleta felt her anger rise. Monticello custom or not, Hortensio's questions were offensive.

"No, of course I haven't," she replied. "Have you, by any chance?"

Hortensio shook his head.

"Is there any physical impediment that you are aware of which would prevent you from having children?"

Aleta's face turned hot with what she knew was a bright red blush.

"These questions seem rather personal," she said quietly but firmly, surprised at her forcefulness.

"I want children very much someday, with the right man, of course. And I don't see any reason why I won't have any. I'm sure you will want children someday, as well, Hortensio," she added, staring defiantly at the prince, who had let his beloved wine list drop to his lap. "Even if you are planning on sacrificing them for the prince, having your own children is a wonderful thing to look forward to."

Hortensio picked up his wineglass and took a long gulp, without once letting his eyes wander from her face.

Giancarlo simply stared. At her.

"There's only one more question," Hortensio said quietly. "And I'm sorry that you feel we are prying. But, *señorita,* surely you can understand that in these days of heightened security, changing mores and a rapidly transforming world we must ask a great many more personal questions of those near His Highness than in earlier times."

"You're asking these questions because of security concerns?"

Hortensio shifted uncomfortably in his seat.

"I guess you could say that," he hedged.

"You've been concerned about security all this time?" Aleta asked. Was it possible that the hostile atmosphere would dissipate once the necessary security check was finished? After all, hadn't she read about the tight security of the most recent Hollywood marriage where the movie-industry guests didn't even know the identity of the superstar bride and groom until after the ceremony?

"Well, go ahead and ask the last question."

"Are you a virgin?"

The question hung in the air like the aftershock of an explosion. Aleta had never been so angry in her life.

But, even as she was livid, she couldn't answer—the question had cut to the inner core of her life, to the part within her that had never known intimacy and yet longed for it. When she had been a junior in high school, Maggie had lost her virginity to her longtime boyfriend and she assured Aleta that nonvirgins could tell if a woman was a virgin by her eyes. Aleta had spent many hours in front of the mirror trying to decide if her eyes were... different.

Could this trio of men know? From her eyes? From the hot blush that she knew was traveling from her forehead down?

Ice cream, sweatpants, a movie on TV and a pair of fuzzy slippers in her own small apartment were looking better and better.

"I don't think that question has anything to do with security," Aleta said quietly, with as much graceful calm as she could muster. "And, if you ask me one more personal question that is as offensive as that, I will leave," she added in the barest whisper. She could hardly believe she had stood up for herself.

Hortensio sputtered an apology.

"I'm sure you find this offensive, *señorita,* and we don't mean in any way to pry, but the personal nature of our mission requires..." he said, starting several more sentences and abandoning them as he didn't seem to be able to explain.

"Just stop, Hortensio," Giancarlo interrupted. "I already know the answer."

"Oh, really?" Aleta asked.

"I can see it in your eyes."

Her mouth flew open, but the hundreds of nasty retorts she wanted to make didn't come out. She wanted to tell him, maybe even at the top of her lungs, that everything the *International Snoop* said about him was true. Rude, aloof, arrogant, disdainful, cold... these were the least of his faults. She stared at him, determined to show him that she couldn't be made to blush, even in the face of his damnably cool stare. She wanted to prove him wrong—even if he wasn't.

But nasty retorts, angry replies, forceful arguments had never come out of her mouth—at least not in the past several years, when the life had gone out of her, gone out of her with her mother's last breath.

She wanted to escape to the warm safety of her apartment, far away from this man who seemed to be able to stare into her most secret heart.

Aleta resolved to ask Maggie just what it was that changed about a woman's eyes. When she had been with a man.

"Why do you care if I'm a virgin?" she asked, ignoring Hortensio's look of warning. "You didn't seem to care when you stole that girlfriend from the prince of Luxembourg—she certainly wasn't a virgin."

"I didn't steal her from—"

"And when you went out with that porno star from England," she added, surprised that she had the audacity to bring up these matters. "You can't persuade me you were worried about whether she was—"

"I was never, never involved with her," he exclaimed, and his eyes flickered with angry flames of passion. "She made up the whole thing."

Hortensio put his head in his hands and heaved a few Spanish oaths that Aleta recognized from when her mother lost at Monopoly, which was often.

"You never cared if that duchess from France was a virgin—she'd been married four times."

Suddenly she was enjoying herself—she did, after all, have all the facts at her fingertips. She had memorized every detail of his life, and the knowledge that had seemed like trivia to be reserved for parlor games was coming in handy. Very handy.

She delighted in the way that he opened up when he was angry, as if in his defenseless moment of passion, he was a man and not a carefully groomed prince!

Giancarlo threw his napkin down onto his plate.

"I never give a damn if someone I'm sleeping with is a virgin! It's the woman I have to marry that I'm concerned about. My lovers..." He nearly spat out the words as Aleta guessed that years of some resentment were finally unleashed. But what sort of resentment? "My lovers—" the prince continued "—my lovers are experienced—not schoolgirls."

Everything stopped.

From the heartbeat within her chest to the movement of the planets.

There was the woman he had to marry.

And then there were his lovers.

"Your Highness, Your Highness," Hortensio soothed. "Let's approach this a little more calmly."

Aleta slumped in her chair and closed her eyes, momentarily shutting out the jumble of the lights of the Pump Room's crystal chandeliers, of the pleadings of Hortensio, of the awful anger of the prince, and of the news that was finally—how had she missed all the signs?—*finally* sinking in. He wanted her all right, wanted her to be his wife. Maybe *wanted* was too strong a word—*she* was the wife that somebody had foisted upon him. To his unmistakable anger.

A culmination of a dream for her, but all the more shocking because it was true. With a terrible twist.

She was Cinderella with a palace to clean so that the prince could party with his bimbos.

Fighting had brought her this, angrily attacking had brought her this. An offhand proposal from a man who was making it all too clear that she was good enough for the stateroom but not good enough—beautiful, glamorous, fun enough—to gain his love.

"Miss Clayton, please have some more champagne."

She opened her eyes to see three pairs of eyes staring at her. Hortensio held her glass out to her. Rudolph held a handkerchief at her side.

Giancarlo held her gaze.

"Señorita, you'll feel so much better with some wine," Hortensio said. "And maybe we can get this . . . courtship off to a better footing."

Ignoring Hortensio, she leaned forward.

"Have to marry?" she whispered, desperately trying to hold back the tears. "As in forced or *required* to marry?"

The prince nodded.

"Yes, exactly that."

"Your Highness, I don't think that this is the best way to approach Miss Clayton," Hortensio warned. "Remember she's the last candidate on this continent."

"But you're not a virgin," Aleta said dismally.

"I don't have to be a virgin," Giancarlo said explosively. "You're the one who has to be a virgin. And, in exchange for that fairly simple requirement, you'll be made a princess. And, in time, a queen. What is wrong with you—don't you want to be a princess?"

"Careful, Your Highness," Hortensio murmured. "Perhaps we should order some dinner."

"Being a princess is not a bad deal," Giancarlo continued, as Aleta stared at her plate. She was powerless to reply, as she was powerless to respond to Mr. McCormick's tirades. The prince took her silence to mean that she was nearly ready to topple, to concede to his wisdom, and his ring. "You'd rule over almost three million subjects, you'd travel the world over as a good-will ambassador for the country, you'd have a wonderful life-style and you'd never have to type a letter or pay the rent again."

"How about the Petrossian caviar on toast points with hard-boiled eggs, onions and vodka shots?" Hortensio suggested, cheerfully attempting to silence the prince by ignoring his tirade. "I think when we have some food in our stomachs, we'll feel a lot better and we can resolve this..."

Sweatpants, ice cream, movie, fuzzy slippers.

Running away was so much better than facing the consequences of the evening.

Aleta rose from her chair. The men fell silent.

"Your Royal Highness, I wouldn't marry you if you were the last man on earth," she blubbered, sounding less like the cold, controlled woman she wanted to be and more like a kindergartner hurt on the playground. "Everything the *Snoop* said about you is true—you're rude and cold, arrogant and spoiled rotten. When you went back up to your room and changed, I thought you might be a nice man. Well, I was wrong. You, Prince Giancarlo, are a jerk!"

With the tears now streaking down her face, she grabbed Maggie's evening bag and slid behind Rudolph to reach the elegant Chinese screen that had shielded them from the stares of other Pump Room customers. When she emerged from the cloistered section, the dining room fell silent and she gasped at the sight of two hundred people staring... at her.

With a hard swallow and a quick swipe at her tear-stained cheeks, she gathered up her skirt and walked with as much dignity as possible toward the door.

She saw that within the hotel lobby, a gaggle of reporters and photographers was lying in wait—ready to pounce.

Aleta turned around.

There was no way she could face them.

Face reporters who would obviously caption a shot of her: Dowdy Woman Prince Forced To Marry.

Then she saw it—across the room.

A fire exit.

Most diners had gone back to their plates, their conversations, their wine. After all, the dinner companion of a prince was considerably less interesting than the prince himself. So, few noticed her slipping toward the fire exit.

Fire Exit.

Open Only In Case of Emergency.

Alarm Will Sound.

Aleta read the signs and hesitated. Some fire exits she had encountered, at school or work, were often disengaged—so there wasn't any way of telling whether she was going to put the restaurant into a panic.

Maybe I should face the reporters, she thought.

But when she turned again, she saw one of the photographers talking with the maitre d'. The maitre d' was pointing to her. All she wanted was the chance to run and hide, to hide within the safety of her quiet and uneventful evenings.

Hesitating only briefly, Aleta took a deep breath and pushed open the steel door.

A lady's scream and a blaring fire bell followed her as she fled to the sidewalk.

"She called me a jerk," Giancarlo said, staring into his wine. "She actually called me a jerk."

"Your Highness, she is only repeating what the media has written about you." Hortensio tried to comfort him.

"That's different. I don't care what the *International Snoop* or any other magazine thinks of me," Giancarlo said. "It's just, why should she think I'm a jerk? And why was she crying? After all, I asked her to marry me. There's a dozen women on several continents who have begged to hear those words from me."

A sudden screech of a fire bell answered him. Hortensio and Rudolph leapt up, and Hortensio pulled a small gun from within his jacket. He nodded at Rudolph, and the taller man disappeared into the dining room, which had erupted with a cacophony of screams, breaking glasses and sirens.

"Your Highness, there has been an alarm," Hortensio shouted over the din. "We have no way of knowing whether there's been a security breach. We must get you out of this dining room."

"She thinks I'm a jerk," Giancarlo repeated, barely noticing his aide. "Any other woman in the world would leap at the chance to marry me—the deposed princess of Yugoslavia threatened suicide because I would not. What on earth can be wrong with Aleta?"

Chapter Three

"Let me get this straight," Maggie began, eyes widened with disbelief. "The most handsome, eligible, titled, wealthy man in all the world asked you to marry him last night and you said no."

Stated this bluntly, Aleta knew that her actions of the night before didn't sound very rational. Nonetheless, there wasn't any way to take the night back. Nor could she explain the evening in a way that Maggie and Rhoda would understand.

Beginning with the prom dress, which she knew she would never discuss with Maggie—it would be too cruel.

And ending with a moment when she realized that standing up for herself, even if it was while she was running away, had been so important to her. She knew that Maggie and Rhoda thought a marriage proposal from a prince meant stars in the sky, champagne in a glass and romance.

They didn't know that this particular marriage proposal was nothing less than a blunt declaration that she wasn't as pretty, as glamorous, as wonderful as the women he had already loved and those he would love if they married.

Her greatest qualification, it had to be admitted, was the fact that she was related by blood to a group of people she didn't even know.

And that she was a virgin, she admitted with a blush.

That last fact, in and of itself, was enough to make her an oddity.

But a princess?

These must be lean times for fairy tales, Aleta considered, *if I'm the heroine. Except I'm in the version of Cinderella where the party girls go out with the prince and I'm stuck making the heirs and cleaning the fireplaces all over the palace.*

This fairy tale was too complicated, too painful to explain.

She simply nodded her head.

"You're right. I said no."

Maggie slumped back in her desk chair as if she were a balloon that had been pricked with a pin.

"But yesterday you were telling us you loved him," Rhoda reminded her. "Aleta, you're not making any sense."

Aleta fidgeted with her calculator, hoping the two women would turn to other subjects. But her friends continued to stare at her, as if hoping that some sort of explanation for her admittedly crazy-sounding behavior would appear on her face.

"By the way, did the figures from the warehouse come in?" Aleta asked with a gulp. "Uh, I have to send out reminder notices to..."

"Get a load of the headlines!"

Like a tornado, Carla burst into the office holding four copies of the *Chicago Tribune.* She dumped three on her desk and held up the fourth.

"Isn't it amazing!" she demanded.

"'Consumer Price Index Down'?" Aleta read, puzzled at Carla's excitement. "Or are you looking at 'Governor To Appear At...'"

"No, you silly goose. This one." She flung the paper onto Aleta's desk. "And check out the picture."

With Carla's finger firmly planted at the margin, Aleta read the midpage headline.

"'Secret Señorita—Monticello Prince Finally Snagged!'"

Aleta gasped as she looked at the picture of herself, arm in arm with the prince—taken as they had walked from the hotel lobby into the Pump Room. He had been caught midscowl by the camera, and now Aleta understood that angry look. How he must despise the constant scrutiny! As for herself, she looked like a rabbit startled and mesmerized by the headlights of an oncoming car.

A rabbit in an evening gown, of course.

A more experienced VIP would have been able to tell her that all the best people—stars, politicians, celebrities—look their worst when caught unawares by the media.

But Aleta wasn't experienced enough to know.

I didn't realize I looked that bad, she thought dismally. *No wonder I'm wife material.*

"Wow! You dined on foie gras, braised pheasant and truffles sautéed in sherry," Maggie reported. The other two women had opened the remaining *Tribunes* and were avidly reading the details of Aleta's evening.

At least, as reported in the press.

"We never got around to eating dinner," Aleta explained, ignoring Maggie's raised eyebrows. "I mean, our evening ended before dinner was served. I ate a grilled cheese sandwich at home."

"You drank imported champagne," Rhoda exclaimed triumphantly. She continued to read, "And you wore a designer gown—the *Tribune* thinks it was a Chanel seen at their show in Paris only last week."

"I knew that dress would be perfect," Maggie said blissfully. "It was marked down half off when I bought it—imagine people thinking it's a Chanel."

Tuning out her friends, Aleta read quickly, skipping over the section devoted to the history of Monticello, which was brief, and list of the prince's previous girlfriends, which wasn't. The article was riddled with errors, creating for the reader an image of a romantic and sensual evening that bore no relation to the cold and calculating conference for which she had been summoned to the Ambassador East's Pump Room.

The humiliation still haunted her.

She was gratified that her identity had not been discovered by the press. For now, she was the "mystery woman" who had stolen the prince's heart. But Aleta could already see that the media was going to be diligent in tracking her down. And discovering things about her.

Everything about her.

Like the fact that she was wife material and anything but a lover.

After all, the article claimed, this mystery woman was now a front runner in "the high stakes race to bring the prince to the altar."

Once the press knew of her identity, Aleta guessed, her life wouldn't be her own. She had read enough *International Snoop* articles to know that every smidgen from her history, every detail of her life, would be known to millions.

Her experiences—and lack of them—would be public knowledge.

Oh, my God, she thought with rising horror, *there's going to be a headline announcing Last Virgin In America Weds Prince.*

That last unsettling thought made her reach for her diet cola. A long gulp settled her nerves slightly as she tried to think of more pleasant alternatives.

Maybe it was better that she had refused him. Within days, hours perhaps, he would be seen with another woman on his arm. The interest in who Aleta was, or who she had been, would evaporate.

At the thought of him, she paused—recognizing the pain within her heart. Why did he have to be so damned handsome, so damned sexy, so damned magnetic? It made it so much harder to remember that a marriage should be based on love.

On two people in love.

Not just one.

Not just one miserable bookkeeper in love with a prince who didn't love her.

Was she making a mistake in refusing him?

After all, her mother had married a man who shared her feelings—running off in a dazzling moment of love, if her story was to be believed, when half a dozen suitably wealthy, well-connected, titled Monticellan men were prepared to join their lives with hers. Three years after her impetuous leap, her mother had been penniless, abandoned and a widowed parent in Chicago. And her family in Monticello had never forgiven her.

Though her mother had never claimed to have regretted her choice, Aleta had often wondered. . . .

Aleta remembered the dreams that had awoken her nearly every hour the night before—dreams of the prince that had begun with steamy, disturbing sensuality that she had never even thought possible, dreams that had ended with humiliations that highlighted that his love, his sexual delight, were reserved for others.

"They think there was an attempt on his life last night!" Maggie announced, having reached the second page of the article more quickly than anyone else. She read the words with gusto. "'Pandemonium erupted in the ordinarily quiet and discreet night spot when sirens pierced the air.'"

Aleta startled.

Had the prince been in any danger last night?

She was surprised by her own reflexive concern.

Stop it! she commanded herself. *He's not the fantasy prince you mooned over as a teenager. He's a cold and calculating, snobbish and insensitive...*

"Oh, it turns out it was just a malfunctioning fire alarm," Maggie explained.

"It wasn't malfunctioning," Aleta said, uncomfortably aware of her office mates' piercing looks. "I set it off. You see, after he asked me to marry him, I ran away through the fire exit. I didn't mean to set it off."

Her friends stared silently at her.

The telephone rang.

Aleta had never been more grateful for an interruption.

"It's some guy," the receptionist announced. "He's on his way back to your office."

The prince? At the thought, Aleta felt her heartbeat quicken with delight. He had reconsidered. He had decided to act as a man and not as a prince. He was going to walk right in here and apologize and they would start their relationship afresh.

The telephone slipped from her hand to her lap as she thought of him and realized that she didn't know whether Giancarlo was the man she had met last night or the man she had followed so avidly with her heart.

Her foolish, wildly romantic heart.

But it wasn't the prince who appeared at the door of the bookkeeping department.

It was Hortensio.

All the excitement drained from Aleta as the small man bowed to each of the office mates in turn—with a last, more profound bow in her direction.

"His Highness has entrusted me with a message requesting your appearance at breakfast this morning," he said. "A car has been provided and..."

"Oh, wow, Aleta, you'd better run!" Rhoda exclaimed. "You're not going to get another chance."

"Yeah, girl, get your jacket," Maggie added.

Aleta stared at her friends and then her eyes returned to the picture of her in the newspaper.

A rabbit in an evening gown.

No gumption.

No spine.

No standing up for herself.

Not with Mr. McCormick and not with a man who looked at her and thought dull. Drab. Wife material, but not lover.

A rabbit in an evening gown.

"No," Aleta said resolutely, turning the page of the paper to an article on yet another South American coup. Anything was better than being reminded that everyone thought of her as someone who could be ordered about.

"What!" Maggie bolted upright in her chair. "You mean, you're not going to go?"

"No," Aleta repeated, keeping her eyes focused on the article about the toppling government. She lifted her chin defiantly. "If the prince thinks that I am one of his subjects who can be ordered about, he's wrong. I'm an American citizen and I have work to do."

"Listen, we'll tell McCormick that you're sick," Maggie said.

"Very sick," chimed in Rhoda.

"If he comes in this morning," Carla added. "I heard his golf game didn't go too well yesterday and he's home pouting."

"Do as the prince desires," Hortensio pleaded. "All he commands is the pleasure of your company."

"If the prince desires my company, he can ask for the pleasure himself," Aleta said, with a tartness that surprised her. She turned to the monthly sales reports with exaggerated concentration.

"You want the prince to come up to this . . . office?" Hortensio asked, looking about the drab, gray room with its institutional furniture and its worn carpet.

Aleta worked hard to keep from looking at the poor aide who, she guessed, dreaded having to inform the prince that a royal command had been refused.

Could she explain how much of the previous evening had been spent crying? How much of the previous evening had been spent wondering if there was something wrong with her—something that made everyone think they could walk all over her? Her boss, the prince, even Maggie when she wanted to borrow a sweater.

Wife material. But not lover material.

Aren't they supposed to be one and the same? She had asked herself that in the privacy of her apartment, in the cover of the darkest night. She had asked herself each time she had awakened.

Not when it's a woman like me, she had answered. *Not when its someone who can't even stick up for herself, who doesn't even have the spark, the feistiness, to fight for her man.*

Her face had stared back, hollowed by the depressing conclusions that had come out of a proposal that had excited her senses when it had been just a fantasy.

"Of course, the prince should come up to the office," Maggie exclaimed suddenly. "After all, we're the closest thing she's got to family—if he wants to go out with her, we have to look him over!"

The other two office mates, the implications dawning on them, nodded in agreement. What a treat it would be to tell everyone that they had met the prince of Monticello . . . in person!

"I mean, we don't know this guy from Adam," Carla said. "He could be an ax murderer or something. A girl can't be too careful these days about who she dates."

Hortensio shook his head.

"Ladies, you don't want him in your office," he said. "You don't know how much you don't want him here. My dear Aleta, please do as the prince commands."

Aleta looked up briefly from the sales figures that danced in front of her eyes. It was precisely the word *commands* that hardened her resolve.

Fantasies are better left as fantasies, she had decided last night—and nothing this morning had changed her mind.

"No, I won't," she said. "The prince may think he's doing me a huge favor asking me to marry him or asking me to see him—and maybe he is. But I am a woman and I will be treated as a woman and not as a subject to be ordered about. If he wants to go out with me, he can ask me himself."

If her voice wavered, if her hands shook, if she was not as decisive as she sounded, no one noticed. Instead, four people stared at her—trying to comprehend the insanity that had possessed her.

But was it insanity? Was it insanity to want a marriage founded on love and not duty? Was it insanity to throw away a marriage such as this would be for the possibility of love to be discovered someday?

Having never experienced love with a man, Aleta had no way of knowing whether she was being foolish and childish—or whether the dictates of her heart were those of maturity.

But she kept her ambivalences to herself and bit her lip.

Hortensio, seemingly cowed by her brave speech and having waited in vain for a retraction, bowed and withdrew. And the office was shrouded in uncomfortable silence. Aleta knew her office mates thought she was crazy—and maybe she was. Crazy to take a stand such as requesting the prince to come up to the office.

Aleta wondered if it would be the last time she would see the diminutive aide to Monticello royalty.

Last night was certainly the last time she would ever see the prince.

Why, oh, why, had she boxed herself into this position of pride? She couldn't honestly say that he wasn't handsome, that he wasn't charming, that he wasn't the sort of man any woman would be happy to claim as her own. That he wasn't the man she wanted, very desperately, to marry.

But to marry with all the love that every bride deserves.

But her mother had anticipated this situation exactly when she had spoken of duty and Aleta's right to be a princess. Had her mother even thought of her as dowdy wife material?

No, Aleta couldn't think of that possibility.

What was wrong with marrying him? What was wrong with taking for herself a life that didn't include bills and bosses and drudgery and struggle? A life of beautiful palaces, cadres of servants and never having to want for anything? Even if it didn't involve him loving her?

Her eyes happened to focus on a crumpled section of the *International Snoop* left in her wastebasket from the night before. Another princess's eyes looked out at her—sad, haunted eyes. It was another interminable article about the possibility of royal divorce. Ten years before, this princess's wedding had been a celebration of a very public fairy-tale romance, but her marriage had degenerated rapidly into one of convenience, duty and royal ceremony.

Marrying for wealth and title and the glamour of a throne wouldn't bring any guarantees.

No guarantees of happiness and contentment and love.

Especially when betrayal had come to a sad-eyed princess who had truly loved her prince. And to a prince who had truly loved his princess. Now these two were the subject of endless speculations from the *International Snoop*.

There were never guarantees.

Never guarantees of love to outlast pomp and ceremony.

And from the beginning, this marriage, between a bookkeeper and a prince, wouldn't be about love.

Even before the grand walk down the aisle, the terms of this royal marriage would be clear.

He didn't love her. He didn't expect to love her. Didn't want to love her. Didn't see any reason to love her.

She shook her head and tried to focus on the sales report in front of her. But concentrating on projections of monthly demand for ¾ inch lead bolts didn't help.

A commotion down the hall was building quickly. Aleta felt her blood run cold as she recognized within the cacophony the persistent questions of reporters, the shouted denials of Hortensio, the brusque commands of the prince.

He was coming!

By the time she had completed that thought, he had arrived, standing in the doorway of the office with a determined look that was knowing and somehow derisive, as if he had warned her of something—a warning that she had ignored by her refusal to follow Hortensio.

For a moment, with their eyes locked in infernal combat, she felt proud and ready to fight his damnable arrogance.

But then she remembered what he could find within her eyes, all the secrets and hidden mysteries that he alone could know. She looked away first, conceding the power he had as a man—not even his power as a prince.

"It's the mystery woman!" A reporter shouted and instantly the office was ablaze with shouted questions and whirring cameras.

The prince shrugged. He stood unbuffeted by the dozen reporters and cameramen scratching their way into the office.

Aleta felt a flush of horror as she realized she had given up her privacy—handed it over, in truth—when she had demanded that Giancarlo himself bring an invitation to breakfast! He had been willing to guard her privacy. Or, at least, he had, by imperial command, not thrown her to the wolves now ravaging her office.

She had been the one to invite the wolves in.

"Excuse me, Miss..." A reporter at her side picked up her nameplate from her desk. "Miss Aleta Clayton, tell me about yourself—starting with your age, your birthplace, your growing-up years...."

"How did you meet the prince?"

"Are you a descendant from one of the five Monticellan families?"

"Has he proposed?"

"Are you in love?"

As if from a great distance, she heard other reporters questioning Maggie, Rhoda and Carla. Maggie was telling an avid audience about the time that she and Aleta were in the sixth-grade play together. A photographer was trying to get the three office mates to pose together and another photographer was at Aleta's feet—instructing her to look in his direction. With a smile, no less.

"Look over here."

"No, look over here—and give us a nice, regal smile."

"Don't be so crabby. Let's have a hearty smile for all of Chicago."

"Hey, our readers in Spain want a decent picture, too!"

Beyond them, beyond them all, the prince stood—unmoving, unsmiling, unwavering. There was only a flicker of emotion when she looked up at him, pleading silently with him from the circle of insistent reporters.

"Hey, is there any way we can get a shot of the two of them together?"

"Holding hands."

"No, with their arms around each other."

"How about a kiss?"

Suddenly Hortensio was there, reaching beneath the elbow of the reporter nearest her to tug at her hand.

"Miss Clayton is unable to grant your requests for an interview at this time," he babbled, as he squeezed her through the crush of bodies. "She will be happy to meet with you at a time to be arranged through the consul general's office. Please make all requests by..."

The reporters, suddenly aware that she had slipped beyond their group, jumped for the door. But by now, Aleta had been shoved by Hortensio into the arms of the prince.

"Let's go!" Giancarlo commanded, grabbing her hand and racing down the hallway.

Aleta obeyed willingly, frankly terrified by the grunting, panting, growling media wolves that ran as a pack after them—cameras, notepads and tape recorders in tow. Hortensio, though short and pudgy, nonetheless had sprinted ahead of the prince and Aleta and he held an elevator door open until the two flung themselves within. As the door closed and Hortensio skillfully blocked any reporters from following their prey, he shouted at the reporters in a frantic mix of Spanish and English.

And then the silence of the elevator enveloped the couple at last.

Their escape had been successful. Aleta found herself shuddering with the unexpressed fear. But it wasn't until she was within Giancarlo's arms that she felt the hot tears that had dropped to her cheek and that now were moist upon his jacket sleeve.

His arms were strong and comforting around her, protecting her from the menacing fervor of those who would intrude upon her. For an instant, she looked up into his face, studying the features that she had known—in pictures, anyway—since she was a child.

Was that somersaulting of her stomach because of his nearness or was it simply because of the rapidly accelerating ride down to the first floor?

Suddenly, without meaning to, she was laughing.

The prince looked puzzled and hurt, and started to pull away from her. But she held fast to him—not yet willing to let go of the moment in his arms.

"What in the devil do you find so amusing now?" he asked.

"My dear prince, do you think you could have found anyone else to marry?" she asked, shaking her head as she laughed. "Isn't there anyone else you could have turned the press on? Aren't there any other suitable women in your broodmare?"

The elevator ground to a halt just as his face turned to utter seriousness.

"There have been others that my country has... approached."

As the door to the elevator glided open, Aleta felt her stomach lurch.

"Others?" she asked, not knowing why the prospect of another woman being qualified for the job of... Monticello princess and mother to the next heir bothered her.

"Oh, sure, there's been others," Giancarlo confirmed as he sped her through the lobby. They vaulted through the revolving doors and raced for a waiting limousine.

As the dark limousine pulled away from the curb, Hortensio—puffing with the exertion of running—reached the door and pounded on the window. A bare instant to allow the aide to climb into the seat next to the driver, and the car raced away. Aleta turned around briefly to see from the rear window Hortensio's disappointed pursuers shouting from the street.

"You must understand, Miss Clayton, that our search has not been very successful because our requirements are so precise," Giancarlo continued. "A woman from Prague, with otherwise perfect credentials, was living with another young man—we couldn't consider her because, as you quite rightly intuited, her beloved might eventually sell his story, a most intimate story, to the *International Snoop*. And a woman from Newfoundland was already married. And another from Cocoa Beach, Florida, had four children and she was only twenty!"

"Definitely not princess material," Aleta said, barely able to suppress her sarcasm. "Have you been to dinner with each of these women?" she asked, although she wasn't entirely sure why she wanted to know.

And not entirely comfortable with how her heart galloped as she waited for his answer.

Giancarlo shook his head.

"We did our research and determined each of these women was not appropriate," he explained. "Hortensio's staff investigated your background and we were ninety-nine percent sure of your answers to the questions we posed to you."

Aleta stared at him, horrified at the unknown invasion of her privacy.

"All the questions were answered with a near-perfect degree of certainty except one," Giancarlo added softly, his heavily lidded stare letting her know which question he meant. "That question's answer I ascertained from your eyes."

The provocative words reminded her that the man was too damned sexy for his own good. Or, more correctly, too damned sexy for Aleta's good. She wanted to touch him—to feel the texture of his lips, the warmth of his hand, the pressure of the muscles in his thigh....

Just looking at him made her long for the type of response that he had made clear was not hers to have.

Flustered, Aleta concentrated on the tumult of Chicago's Loop—its most congested business district— which passed before her as the limousine glided effortlessly through traffic. She couldn't, just wouldn't, admit that one of the things she had done when she got home the evening before had been to study her reflection in the mirror—searching for the evidence of her...inexperience.

She had wondered if the lack of experience was what made her unappealing as a lover.

"What about Monticello women? There must be plenty of suitable women living there. Descendants of the five families and all that."

"There's not a virgin among them," Giancarlo said dismissively. "If I married one of the girls I grew up with, I'd be paying half a dozen men for their silence."

Suddenly the enormity of the situation bore down upon her.

It wasn't very pleasant to think about.

"I'm the proverbial last woman on earth, aren't I?" she asked.

Chapter Four

Ay Caramba! Now you've done it, Giancarlo thought to himself with a grimace.

With Hortensio twisted about in his seat in order to scowl at him, and Aleta at his side with her eyes blazing with fury, Giancarlo could not delude himself that the courtship of the future princess of Monticello was going well. Not going well, he chuckled grimly—it was actually turning out to be an unmitigated disaster.

Not that he would care, under ordinary circumstances.

All right, he admitted to himself, she was pretty, even enchanting, and under the most ordinary of circumstances, he would have had no qualms at seducing her. In fact, he would have taken enormous pleasure at loosening the top button on her demure schoolgirl blouse—that button was so very high, and followed by so many more. He would have delighted at pulling her hair from its plain ribbon, feeling its length caress him, feeling its richness respond to his fingers. He would have thrilled at reaching beneath her oh-so-sensible skirt to the soft skin....

On the other hand, even if it were under ordinary circumstances, he wasn't sure he would want the responsibility of deflowering a young girl, of watching her private transformation into a woman. And taking the very public consequences. For all his deserved reputation as a rake, taking advantage of virgins wasn't something Giancarlo would do.

Even in ordinary circumstances.

And these weren't ordinary circumstances.

Ordinary circumstances would have been so different.

From the moment he had entered the exclusive Swiss prep school at thirteen, women had pursued him. Courtship was merely a matter of choosing, of snapping his fingers, of commanding an aide to arrange a tryst.

Actresses, models, singers and stars. Duchesses, marchionesses, and ladies-in-waiting. Girls from good families, girls with fine breeding. Married, divorced, widowed, single—it seemed to make no difference and so often he had found himself in the embarrassing situation of fending off women attached to his own friends.

Women he had never met, would never meet, sent the palace letters accompanied by the most intimate photographs. Women engineered "accidental" encounters, plotting to snare the most eligible bachelor of Europe. Many—those who underestimated his commitment to Monticello and his understanding of his responsibility in marrying the right woman—deluded themselves with the dream of marrying Giancarlo.

But many more women recognized reality and were content with his affection. And several, not satisfied with his renowned generosity at the end of a relationship, had sold their stories to the media—only inflaming his worth in the sensual marketplace.

Lately he had found himself bored with the game—to call it the chase as other men did would be to suggest that it was he who did the pursuing. But the opposite was always the case.

Very, very few were the women who did not respond to him, who did not pursue him, either openly or more covertly—in fact, sitting now in the limousine observing the way that Aleta's lips tightened with anger, Giancarlo couldn't remember any.

But, as he reminded himself yet again, these were not ordinary circumstances.

Aleta was the one woman who was capable of wearing the crown.

She represented duty, country, responsibility, maturity, dynastic continuity and an end to the last remaining vestige of his personal freedom.

Definitely not ordinary circumstances.

"If I might make a suggestion, Your Highness," Hortensio said, interrupting his thoughts, "you could apologize to the *señorita*. Your suggestion that she is the last on the list of women you can consider marrying is a suggestion not normally associated with successful courtship."

"Look here, Hortensio. I don't have any trouble with women," Giancarlo pointed out. "And besides, this isn't courtship—at least, not in the usual terms. This is marriage. A very important dynastic marriage. And besides, she's being very difficult!"

"Difficult!" Aleta shrieked. "You're the one who wants to get married. In America, people who want to bargain with someone have to show the other person what's in it for them."

Giancarlo's face flushed red with anger. Of all the impertinent, utterly presumptuous women! She was completely disregarding all rules of protocol by screaming at him.

"Let's get one thing straight. I don't want to get married. As for what's in it for you, I'm offering you what any other woman in the world would snap up in an instant and be grateful for," he explained. "Wealth, a title, security, a principality to call your own—what more can you want?"

"Love," Hortensio interjected calmly, and his startling injection of the concept silenced the back-seat combatants. "A decidedly American concept—or, at least, a concept that's never been a particularly strong component of dynastic marriages such as this one would be."

The two star-crossed lovers stared out their respective windows, pointedly watching the passing Chicago scenery with resentful quiet. Hortensio sighed heavily and turned around to make some whispered instructions to the driver.

Giancarlo glanced at the woman at his side. Or rather, he stared at the back of her head—since she was studiously avoiding him.

While standing at the balcony of his penthouse suite, regarding the twinkling lights of the sprawling city, he had thought about her throughout the night. At first he had asked himself the question, *What is wrong with Aleta?* There were many things wrong with her—she was too quiet, she didn't hold her head high enough and she wore the most intriguingly inappropriate clothes. No, finding things wrong with her, as he warred with his dutiful side, wasn't the problem. Rather, it was a matter of determining the mystery of why she wouldn't marry.

And marry quietly, with not so much damned fuss.

But later, as the night wore on, he had found himself faced with his most profound insecurities.

Was he really a jerk, like she'd said?

Certainly he had never been told that before. Women found him witty and charming, gracious and sexy—or at least that's what they said. And how they acted. Although, sometimes, at the very end of a relationship, as he faced the fact that he had somehow found an emptiness within a woman's arms, women accused him of many things.

Coldness.

Distance.

An unwillingness to become intimate.

All things he was perfectly happy to confess to—but with another woman so willing to fill in the shoes of the last, these were never accusations or confessions he considered for very long.

The limousine had rolled to a stop in the center of an alleyway, squeezing through a column of garbage Dumpsters.

"Where are we?" Giancarlo asked. "I believe I instructed you to deliver us..."

"Your Highness, I must request a private audience," Hortensio explained. "Could we perhaps step outside?"

Giancarlo glanced at Aleta, but her shrug suggested that she didn't have any better clue as to what was on

Hortensio's mind. Giancarlo followed Hortensio from the car.

"What's on your mind?" he asked, as Hortensio jumped up to sit on the hood of the sleek limousine.

"Women, Your Highness," Hortensio said. "I think I need to impart to you some advice about women. The fairer sex."

Giancarlo roared with laughter.

"Hortensio, I hardly think that you can give me advice about women. After all, haven't I been *International Scoop*'s most eligible bachelor for five years running?"

"That, my dear Prince, is precisely the point," Hortensio explained. "You see, Giancarlo, if you were not a prince, if you were not wealthy and handsome, if you were not titled, would women be attracted to you?"

"Of course not."

"Well, doesn't that bother you?"

Giancarlo leaned up against the car to join his friend as they stared down the length of the alley at some children playing kickball. Their laughter, their boisterous joy in the spring morning, reminded Giancarlo of the soccer games of his youth....

And the boys who were brought to play with him by fathers who were convinced that a friendship with the prince would bode well for their sons' futures. The boys who deferred, with reluctance, because their fathers had commanded it. The unnatural friendships, almost touching in their falsity, had lasted—if only because Giancarlo was gifted in maintaining a studious impartiality with each of his "chums."

Would any of those children have played with him, let him continually be the captain of their teams, if he hadn't been a prince?

"No, it doesn't bother me," Giancarlo said, with a conviction he wasn't sure he felt. "What bothers me is that I should be meeting at this very minute with representatives from the International Bank of Chicago to finalize our economic development plans. I thought I could fit in breakfast with that damnable American who is this minute sitting in our car acting as if she were the princess and I were the commoner."

"What you should be doing with your morning is enjoying the sunshine, enjoying the clear spring air and enjoying the beautiful woman who is sitting in your limousine feeling very much like a discarded piece of junk and not at all like a future princess."

Giancarlo kicked at a rock beneath his feet.

"I'm getting married because of you," he exclaimed. "Because of you, my mother, the parliament, my cabinet and a treaty with Spain—all reasons that have nothing to do with sunshine, fresh air, spring, love or her."

The two men sat in silence. For an instant, momentarily stopped from performing official functions, Giancarlo was aware of the sun that touched the back of his head. He was aware of the fresh, moist spring air that gusted from the lake. He was aware of the laughter of the children and their excited whoops of joy as they skidded and leapt and chased each other.

"I guess this hasn't been a lot of fun for you," Hortensio said. "Looking for a wife, that is."

"No, it hasn't. I have a lot of responsibilities to my country and this is simply another one. Perhaps the least enjoyable one."

"It doesn't have to be."

"You can't say it's been enjoyable so far," Giancarlo reminded Hortensio, pointing briefly back to the limousine. "I've been called a jerk, I've been told she wouldn't marry me if I was the last man on earth, I've had to evade the press with even more than usual..."

"Yet you need her."

"Yes, unfortunately, I need her," Giancarlo said, wondering just how much his need for her encompassed him.

"Perhaps you could court her the way you did the princess of Luxembourg. I was in service to your mother at the time, but I heard you were quite successful at laying siege to the princess—if I could use such a metaphor. Whatever you did there might work with Miss Clayton. You could successfully marry and then..."

The aide shrugged, as if to suggest that once the marriage was complete, the prince would be free. More of a free man than he was this very morning.

"I sent a note to the princess on the eve of the ball to celebrate her father's official birthday and she arrived at my suite within the hour. There wasn't much to it."

"You're right. Somehow I don't think it would work in this case," Hortensio agreed solemnly. Then his face brightened. "What about that Argentinian woman— you know, the prime minister's daughter? You met her when you went on your Latin American goodwill tour. I remember the stink that was raised by the *Snoop* at that. She was, after all, engaged to the son of the ambassador from Brazil."

Giancarlo winced at the memory and then shook his head.

"She had sent me fourteen letters of a rather intimate nature before the tour. She even enclosed some...pictures of herself. When we finally met on the polo fields—" Giancarlo looked at Hortensio, and was

surprised and annoyed by his aide's rapt attention
"—well, when we finally met, there wasn't much of
what one could call courtship."

Stymied, Hortensio clucked in sympathy.

"You are rather in a pickle, Your Highness. Perhaps
you would now be willing to entertain a few sugges-
tions from me."

"From you?"

"I have some success with the ladies," Hortensio declared, throwing back his shoulders. "I don't have your
looks, your title, your wealth or your height—but I
don't do badly. And if I can have success without these
things, think what you can do with my methods and
your attributes."

Giancarlo regarded his aide with renewed interest.
Then his eyes narrowed with suspicion.

"What kind of success have you had with women?"
Giancarlo asked.

Hortensio shook his finger.

"Rule number one—never discuss your past suc-
cesses."

Giancarlo smiled, and looked away. Obviously, he
could ignore Hortensio's ludicrous boasting as well as
any of his ludicrous "rules."

But Hortensio wasn't so easily put off.

"Rule number two—make a woman feel like a queen.
Find out what she wants to do and do it. Find out what
she wants to talk about and listen. Find out how she
wants to be touched and . . ."

"Just give me rule number three," Giancarlo
snapped. Having Hortensio as a romantic adviser was
such a new twist that Giancarlo could hardly believe he
had even listened to this much.

"Ah, Your Highness, I'm afraid I will just this once break rule number one," he said with a mysterious smile. "But only long enough to tell you that I've never had to think of a rule number three because I'm so diligent about following rule number two."

Giancarlo stared with utter surprise at the diminutive aide from head to toe.

"Can you break rule number one long enough to give me some examples?"

Hortensio shook his head.

"I believe we'd better move on," he explained, pointing back to Aleta, who had stepped out of the limousine.

"Are we going somewhere or are you guys negotiating a new arms-reduction treaty?" she asked.

"All right, all right, we're going," Giancarlo conceded, reminding himself that later he would have to talk more about these two rules of love that his aide-de-camp had devised.

In the limousine, Giancarlo considered his choices.

"We will have breakfast at the—"

"Your Highness," Hortensio interrupted. "You're forgetting rule number two."

"Rule number two?" Giancarlo asked, not a little irritated at his aide's presumption.

"What's rule number two?" Aleta chimed in.

Hortensio took a deep breath, ready to explain to his beloved prince.

"Don't bother," Giancarlo said. "I remember."

He turned to Aleta, whose cold-as-ice expression didn't bode well for this royal first.

"Miss Clayton, where would you like to have breakfast?" Giancarlo asked, barely able to disguise his discomfort.

Hortensio beamed—his student was a quick study!

Aleta simply stared, her mouth forming a small, round O of surprise. Her features softened, her eyes losing their sharpness and instead glistening like the finest diamonds.

"You asked me where I wanted to go," she whispered. "You asked me."

Giancarlo shrugged his shoulders.

"Of course I asked you. I've never been the kind of man to..."

"Your Highness."

"What is it, Hortensio?"

"Rule number one."

"Oh, yes, of course. Miss Clayton..."

"Aleta."

Giancarlo did a double take. So Hortensio's methods worked.

Maybe he did have some special lessons to pass on.

If Hortensio was right, he could get this marriage business over with quickly and then...well, try to carve out some personal freedoms later.

"Aleta," Giancarlo repeated. "Aleta, my car is yours. Where may I take you to breakfast?"

Every single one of the booths and tables at Sid and Estelle's deli were taken, filled with chattering north-side workers enjoying an early lunch at the popular, inexpensive hangout. Aleta happily led the prince, Hortensio and the chauffeur to the line of people waiting to get a seat.

"Table in just a minute, honey!" Estelle chirped as she passed Aleta, balancing four plates of potato pancakes on her arms. "Haven't seen ya in a while—glad ya stopped in."

Aleta beamed and then waved to the balding man behind the grill.

"Hi, doll," Sid said, brandishing his spatula.

Giancarlo regarded the confusion of the crowded restaurant.

"Hortensio," he said, "inform the owners of my identity and get us a table immediately."

Aleta spun around, horrified at his suggestion.

"You can't do that here!"

Giancarlo looked at her. It was the first time in his life that someone who was not ahead of him in the immediate succession to the throne of Monticello, namely the queen, had spoken to him that way. And, frankly, the queen never spoke like this, either.

He had a good mind to forget this courtship business and...

"Rule number two," Hortensio whispered at his ear. "Remember rule number two."

Giancarlo sighed.

"All right. We'll wait for a table."

As it was, they didn't have to wait long. Within seconds, two tables opened up. Aleta and Giancarlo took one by the window and Hortensio and the driver took a booth by the grill.

As Estelle placed menus, water glasses and silverware before them, Giancarlo allowed his shoulders to relax. Clearly, he was never going to get to his meeting with the bank and he was never going to finish half a dozen other pressing royal obligations.

On the other hand, maybe it would be fun to take a day off.

Contrary to *International Snoop* reports of his escapades, Giancarlo hadn't had a day off from ribbon cutting, hospital visiting, bank meetings and goodwill tours in several months.

"I'm glad that you waited for a table," Aleta said softly after Estelle finished setting up their table. "It would have made me feel embarrassed otherwise."

Their eyes met, and Giancarlo felt for the first time that he was starting to understand this contrary and exciting woman. Stripping him of a title, of wealth, of his country, she was determined to reach to the man within him.

A man very much hidden from others.

There was something very terrifying about being regarded without the trappings that adorned and advantaged his life. There was something very terrifying about the possibility of being found wanting.

On the other hand, there was something very... intriguing and odd...

About being found right.

"Are you going to sit there mooning at her all day, young man, or are you going to order?" a feminine voice bellowed in his ear.

Estelle, a woman who would only admit to being fifty—and had been admitting that for nearly twenty years—was at his side, holding her order pad with her pen poised.

Giancarlo looked at Aleta and then at his menu. He had never seen a menu such as this one. Finer restaurants had restrained lists of appetizers, soups, salads, entrées and desserts. Sid and Estelle's had a hodgepodge of literally hundreds of combinations of pastrami and corned beef, liver and tongue, Swiss cheese and rye breads. To say nothing of potato pancakes, blinis, soups and...

"What are you having?" he asked Aleta.

"Pastrami with Swiss on rye," she answered. "With mustard."

"I'll take it," he said, handing his menu to Estelle.

"Is this your first time in a deli?" Aleta asked, after Estelle had disappeared to loudly pass along their order to her husband.

Giancarlo nodded.

"So you're a virgin, too."

Giancarlo startled and then smiled at her rather oddly charming comment.

"I suppose I am."

She leaned over the table, resting her head in her hands.

"Have you ever been to a baseball game?"

"No," he confessed. "Although, come to think of it, I once threw out the first pitch at a game in Tokyo, but had to leave before the beginning of the second inning because I had to meet with the emperor."

"So you've never eaten hot dogs and drunk beer in the bleachers?"

He shook his head.

"Ever go to the zoo?"

He considered her question.

"Well, some friends of ours—Greek shipping people—bought their own private zoo for a daughter. Had a lot of interesting animals."

"But you haven't been to a zoo, eaten cotton candy, thrown peanuts at the gorillas and bought a balloon shaped like a giraffe's head?"

"I guess that's right."

"And I suppose you've never gone to the beach."

"Wait just a minute," he said indignantly. "We have plenty of beaches in Monticello and the royal family has its own private one as well as its own fleet of boats and a cabana that was built in the nineteenth century.''

Her eyes twinkled with delight. The damnable woman wasn't going to give an inch.

''Yeah, but you've never gone to Chicago's Oak Street Beach, laid out your towel next to strangers, played in the volleyball games and eaten Sno-Kones.''

''Now would you mind telling me what all this is leading to?''

She laughed.

''It looks like the day is wasted for me, at least as far as going back to the office,'' she said cheerfully. ''And I'd bet the day is shot for you, too. I was thinking I'd be willing to spend the day with you.''

He stared at her in disbelief, and he ignored Estelle as she set plates piled high with food before them.

Willing to spend the day with me?

Giancarlo repeated the phrase to himself, regarding this woman who was breaking all the rules of his life.

Willing to spend the day with me.

''I'm not saying I'll marry you,'' Aleta said, biting into her pickle. She chewed reflectively and swallowed. ''And I'm not saying I'll even see you again. But we could go to the beach.''

''The beach?'' Giancarlo repeated. Suddenly he remembered half a dozen meetings and conference calls and appearances that would have to be rescheduled.

''Well?''

''Sure. Let's go,'' he agreed, biting into his sandwich.

''First get rid of Hortensio.''

Giancarlo's eyes widened as he nearly choked on his food.

"I don't mean anything bad," Aleta hastily added. "I mean, I like Hortensio. It's just I don't really want your chaperon today."

Reflexively, Giancarlo's eyebrows lifted. The playboy within him couldn't be stopped—even if he was with a woman who represented imprisonment by marriage. He was surprised at how his insouciant gesture flattered her, disarmed her, let her natural smile erase the tensions that she had displayed since the moment he had met her when she'd agonized over her inappropriate appearance.

What a beautiful woman, he thought despite himself.

"No, Giancarlo no." She laughed. "Just the beach. We don't need a chaperon for that."

Chapter Five

When the couple slipped out of Sid and Estelle's, Hortensio was left to pay the bill and Aleta learned something about royalty that the *International Snoop* had never told her.

Princes don't carry money.

"Never?"

"Never," Giancarlo confirmed. "That's what we have commoners for."

Aleta looked at him in horror, ready to give him a good, sound lecture on democratic values. His arrogance, his princeliness was getting just a little out of control. Why, she had a mind to...

She saw the devilish twinkling in his eyes as confirmation that he was joking.

"Actually, I'm not quite sure why I've never carried money," Giancarlo explained, following her as she turned down Clybourn Avenue. "Aides have always handled matters such as bill-paying and tipping. I have no idea what the price of breakfast was and wouldn't even be able to guess.''

"But we better be thankful that you don't carry money because that was the only way we were out of Hortensio's sight for a second,'' Aleta said, suddenly recognizing the wistful tone in his voice. Was it possible that some of the privileges of royalty carried with them a price tag of freedom? After all, how it must chafe at a man to have his financial affairs handled by others. Even if those financial affairs were literally billions.

"He's probably still arguing with Estelle about how much the bill was,'' she finished lamely.

"I feel guilty leaving him there,'' Giancarlo said, taking her arm into his. It was a simple gesture of chivalry and manners, and yet, for Aleta, the touch of his skin was a palpable reminder of how the emotional distance between them was being bridged. "This is the first time I've abandoned him since I was thirteen and left him at the train station in Gstaad, Switzerland. I had arrived at the boarding school for the first time—Hortensio had to call in Interpol, the international police. Everyone was convinced there had been a kidnapping.''

There was no way that Hortensio would confuse his prince's morning escape with a kidnapping. Though he had shouted after Giancarlo and Aleta as they left the deli, he was powerless to chase them with Estelle's determined hand clutching his.

After all, the bill had to be paid.

"He's with you all the time?''

"He serves a security function, as well,'' Giancarlo said. "He's small but he's got a black belt in some Eastern martial art and he's an expert marksman.''

Aleta shivered though the spring air was warm and inviting. The thought of security details coupled with the long history of political assassinations made her realize that his life as a prince was fraught with danger and circumscribed by ceremony and responsibility.

After sharing a hot dog from Sammy's Red Hots, Aleta and Giancarlo walked through Water Tower Place, Chicago's elegant shopping mall. And after that they rode the Streeterville bus to the Navy Pier. Park District workers were trimming the trees that lined the boulevard through the park that had once been a navy installation. The breezes from the lake chilled Aleta, and the prince gave her his jacket.

Gradually, in increments too small to be counted, the prince became a more relaxed, more cheerful companion. He delighted in the novelty of his experience. As Aleta had guessed, he had never done the half a dozen things that an average Chicagoan does in a perfectly average morning.

"Tell me about your average day, your perfectly normal day—you can't spend every morning like this," he said, as they approached the beach. A few brave sun worshipers, playing hooky from work or school, looked up as Giancarlo and Aleta passed.

"That's the kind of question you would ask me if we'd been married five years," Aleta teased, thinking that the conversation would drift to other things. She felt self-conscious at his interest—and surprised at the longing with which he said the words *normal* and *average*.

What an enormous, cavernous distance between their lives. It was a wonder they could talk to each other at all.

"I'm just a bookkeeper," she pointed out. She wondered at the glamour that must be part of his every day, his "average" days. "My life is pretty boring compared to what yours must be like."

Giancarlo shook his head, and for an instant, Aleta's heart went out to him.

He looked so sad, and so thoughtful.

"I like to hear about the lives of other people," he explained. "I know I seem aloof and arrogant—" he held his hand up to silence her protests "—but that's the way we royals are. We feel, we long for things, we have wants just as other people do. We have disappointments, too," he added. And though his words were general, Aleta knew there were specific disappointments, specific frustrations he was thinking of. "And we feel that we don't have the freedom that we want, that there's too many things we have to get done, too many things others want from us—I feel those things the same as any person does."

"Really?" she asked. "Tell me about those disappointments, those frustrations."

He looked at her, for a moment caught with his emotional armor unworn. But he was too strong a man, had been so long the one to whom others turn, to withstand his own vulnerability. For a scant second, his eyes were clear, he was a man and not a title. But then his coolness, his calm, returned.

"I must plead royal privilege and ask you to tell me about you—the day before Monticello called," he said.

She shivered, not knowing whether it was because of the tenuous intimacy that had almost, but not quite, developed between them or because of the brisk lake wind that gusted about and tugged at her skirt.

He should have, would have kissed her. After all, she was the woman he wanted for his bride. But it was the very word *wanted* that stopped him. He didn't want her or any other bride, didn't want any wedding, didn't want the ceremony that would cut him off from the only autonomy he had within his responsibilities as prince to three million citizens. Each citizen looking to him to maintain and enhance their way of life.

"I picked up a box of Pop Tarts and a Diet Coke at the White Hen down the street from my apartment," Aleta said, breaking the awkward silence by returning to the relatively neutral topic of her daily routine.

What could account for the sudden change within him? She was too young, too inexperienced, to recognize the moment when a man sees his own needs, his own weakness for a woman. But she was empathetic enough to understand that he had remembered something, in that moment when any other man would have kissed her. *He remembered who I am—the wife material,* she thought dejectedly.

I'm not going to let this ruin my day, she resolved, tilting her chin defiantly. *I'm not going to let how he thinks of me change the delight I feel at a day away from the office, with a man who will, in these brief hours, give me the memories for my grandchildren. Or for myself.*

She pressed ahead with her account of the day before yesterday, the day before her life had been turned upside down by a prince.

"I usually eat Pop Tarts for breakfast, even though I know I should eat more healthy foods. And I'm sure that Diet Coke isn't all that good for you in the morning. Juice would be better. But I picked up a package of

NO COST! NO OBLIGATION TO BUY!
NO PURCHASE NECESSARY!

PLAY "LUCKY 7"
AND GET AS MANY AS SIX FREE GIFTS...

HOW TO PLAY:

1. With a coin, carefully scratch off the silver box at the right. This makes you eligible to receive two or more free books, and possibly other gifts, depending on what is revealed beneath the scratch-off area.

2. You'll receive brand-new Silhouette Romance™ novels. When you return this card, we'll send you the books and gifts you qualify for *absolutely free!*

3. If we don't hear from you, every month, we'll send you 6 additional novels to read and enjoy. You can return them and owe nothing but if you decide to keep them, you'll pay only $2.25* per book, a saving of 44¢ each off the cover price. There is **no** extra charge for postage and handling. There are **no** hidden extras.

4. When you join the Silhouette Reader Service™, you'll get our subscribers'-only newsletter, as well as additional free gifts from time to time just for being a subscriber.

5. You must be completely satisfied. You may cancel at any time simply by sending us a note or a shipping statement marked "cancel" or by returning any shipment to us at our cost.

This lovely heart-shaped box is richly detailed with cut-glass decorations, perfect for holding a precious memento or keepsake—and it's yours absolutely free when you accept our no-risk offer.

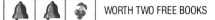

SILHOUETTE "NO RISK" GUARANTEE

- You're not required to buy a single book—ever!
- You must be completely satisfied or you may cancel at any time simply by sending us a note or a shipping statement marked "cancel" or returning any shipment to us at our cost. Either way, you will receive no more books; you'll have no obligation to buy.
- The free books and gifts you receive from this "Lucky 7" offer remain yours to keep no matter what you decide.

If offer card is missing, write to: Silhouette Reader Service, 3010 Walden Ave., P.O. Box 1867, Buffalo, NY 14269-1867

DETACH AND MAIL CARD TODAY

frosted cherry ones and a can of Diet Coke at the White Hen on my way to the bus stop.''

'' 'White Hen'?''

''Oh, that's the convenience store down the street from where I live,'' she explained. He still looked baffled. ''It's like a little grocery store.''

''Ah, I see,'' he nodded. ''And 'Pop Tarts'?''

''It's a breakfast pastry. There are six in a box. I really like the cherry ones. I usually keep a box in my desk so that I can have breakfast when I get to the office. Sort of a last bit of peace and quiet before the bills and orders take over.''

As they walked along the cement embankment that separated Lake Michigan from Lake Shore Drive, the conversation never strayed. Giancarlo wanted to know about everything. The bus ride to work. What Maggie had talked about in the morning—her date of the previous evening, of course. The accounting system used at McCormick and her boss's temper tantrums. The gossip about Rhoda's cousin, who was pregnant again.

Giancarlo was attentive and intrigued by everything—for the first time in her life, Aleta felt that each word she said was really listened to. Or perhaps the second time, since her mother had often been that attentive to her stories about her school days.

He only interrupted to ask more questions and Aleta noted that his laughter at the more amusing parts of her routine was quick and unrestrained, so very different from the controlled mask that he ordinarily presented. Without noticing it, they had abandoned the formality and distance that would have characterized a first date.

A first date with a prince.

A first unchaperoned date, because Aleta had to admit that their first dinner had been a date, as well.

Admittedly, a very bad one.

"Why don't you tell me about your day?" she asked, suddenly embarrassed by the way in which she had monopolized the conversation for the past hour.

"Boring, very boring," he said dismissively. He motioned to a series of concrete steps that led from the lake to the tunnel through the busy Lake Shore Drive.

Sitting down on one of the steps, Aleta pressed him again to describe his day.

"After all, it's only fair," she teased. "Besides, I never get to do half the things you do—remember, I work for a living. Just to hear about the fun things you must do all day long..."

His eyes clouded over and, for an instant, Aleta thought he wouldn't answer. Then he took a deep breath, and, with his eyes trained on a trio of kids playing at the edge of the water, listed off the responsibilities of a prince—the Tuesday responsibilities of a prince from Monticello.

"I began my day at the First Bank of Chicago where I met with the development office to work out final details on a Monticello construction project that will use some Chicago contractors and subcontractors—it's part of my pet project to use international contacts to develop our country. After the meeting, I spoke at the University Club—a fifty-minute talk to businessmen on the importance of international commercial cooperation. Then a photo opportunity with the mayor and a delegation of public school teachers who will be traveling to Monticello next year for a tour of our schools. Then a meeting with restorative architects to discuss our most famous cathedral and damage being done to it by pollution. I want very much to negotiate a fair price for the work, one that won't require increased taxes for my citizens.''

"And then you had dinner with me?" Aleta asked, awed by the sheer volume of work he had accomplished.

He laughed, although he never took his eyes from the children, who had now decided to tentatively wade into the lake.

"Then I had breakfast."

He looked at her now, and smiled at her incredulity. But all she could think was that if his "perfectly normal" day included these duties, her day included a lot fewer hassles than his did.

Even if you threw in a half-dozen Mr. McCormicks.

"Well, at least you got to relax during breakfast."

"I had my breakfast with one of this city's leading industrialists," he added, "who is trying to find new places to invest—I hope he chooses my country, and I spent my time over eggs Benedict persuading him to do just that."

"Aren't you being a little greedy?" Aleta teased. "After all, you're pretty wealthy."

He shook his head and Aleta sensed his exasperation. His world was so foreign, his concerns so much different from her own.

"I may be wealthy—but it is wealth that belongs to Monticello. As for greed, I call it service to my people. I am responsible for giving them the best possible opportunities and the best possible resources. That's what the nobility was always meant to do. Although history is full of kings, queens and princes who abused their positions."

"Sounds like a lot of work," Aleta said, not sure if she believed herself. After all, weren't there aides and ministers and cabinet officials who were supposed to take care of the dirty jobs while a prince frolicked?

"There are three million Monticellans living in my country and hundreds of thousands more all around the world," Giancarlo continued. "I'm responsible for every one. Royalty was never meant to just play."

"But you do." Aleta pointed out, letting her gaze fasten on his face. The rugged lines of his face were tense and, as she followed his watchful eyes to the water, she realized he was nervous about the children—they couldn't be any more than ten years old—as they waded deeper into the water.

"You do play a lot," Aleta continued, sensing even as she spoke that he wasn't fully attentive. But she was determined to press him on what she knew were the facts. "You ski at Gstaad, you play polo in Argentina, and just last week, I saw the photos of you at a party in the Hamptons."

"I take an afternoon off and the press makes it out to be a two-week frolic. I engage in sports with heads of state to be able to negotiate deals for my country in less antagonistic circumstances, and I'm accused of frolicking. I agree to attend a charity event because my very presence will ensure higher ticket sales and I'm accused of frittering away my time at parties."

His mouth was open, ready to say more, and Aleta sensed he was unleashing resentments he had kept to himself for years.

But he would never begin that sentence.

Aleta heard a scream from the lake, high-pitched and frantic. It was joined by other shouts of terror.

She saw a bare flash of movement as Giancarlo flung off his shoes and leapt toward the water, his white broad cloth shirt and silk tie abandoned on the cement embankment.

And, in the water, she saw the catastrophe that the prince had watched for, had anticipated while she had been blissfully unaware of danger.

Two of the children who had been playing in the water were waist-deep in the lake. Panicked and crying, jogging through the deepening water, the two children drew her eyes—and made her think, for a moment, that the prince was headed in the wrong direction—farther out in the lake.

But then her eyes were drawn to the more dangerous problem. A third child had ventured out too far, and his recklessness had been rewarded by disaster. Fallen from a water shelf, the boy gulped at the water, screaming for help and then bobbing back down into the deep, into silence.

Aleta knew that the water at the edge of the cement looked disarmingly shallow—but the first ten feet of wading was a deadly invitation to a drop of nearly twenty feet of murky water infested with strong grasses and weeds that could tangle around a hapless victim's legs. A victim who, like too many city kids, had never been taught to swim.

The prince was nearing the boy, gliding with strong, even strokes.

Aleta felt herself relax, and was only then aware of how long she had held her breath. Surely all would end well.

Except the two other children now panicked, and, thinking they were being helpful, headed for their buddy—not realizing that they, too, would meet the deadly water ledge and be helpless in its wake.

How would Giancarlo be able to bring all three boys back to safety?

"Stop! Get back! It's too deep!" Aleta screamed, but her voice couldn't carry over the shrieks of the boys struggling against the water.

Aleta yanked off her shoes and threw off Giancarlo's jacket onto the pile of his own discarded wear. Behind her, she heard the squeal of tires as a few Lake Shore Drive riders recognized the emergency.

"Is there something I can do?" a voice shouted from behind her.

"Call for help!" she cried and then, steeling herself against the frigid rush of water, dove in.

Her last conscious thought was that she had never meant to be a hero, but she wasn't the kind of person who became one.

Heroism was for others, fighting was for those who could withstand the battle.

But then there were the boys.

The instinct took over, ready to battle the water, the cold and three terrified children.

The boys were lucky—so very lucky.

They were so lucky, in fact, that the police felt justified giving a lengthy lecture—a lecture they might not have had the heart for if things hadn't turned out so well. A lecture on the evils of skipping school, on the foolishness of playing in the lake when there were no lifeguards in sight and on the stupidity of wading out in unfamiliar water.

"What does this sign say?" An officer demanded for the umpteenth time, pointing his nightstick to the No Swimming sign that was painted on the cement embankment.

Aleta smiled as she heard each of the boys read the sign—and read it several more times to the officer's satisfaction.

"They're sure going to remember this morning," she said.

"God, so am I," Giancarlo muttered. "That water was damned cold—whatever possessed them to play in it?"

"That's just how boys are, I guess."

Side by side under a scratchy wool Chicago Police Department blanket, the two sipped coffee from disposable cups a harried fireman had handed them. Surrounded by ambulances, squad cars and a fire truck— all of which had thankfully turned out unnecessary— Aleta and Giancarlo were pretty well ignored on their perch on the very same cement step they had had to themselves a half hour before. Police officers, paramedics, firemen and a crowd of curious civilians milled about.

"How did you do it?" Aleta asked. "How did you manage to bring that kid in?"

"How did *we* do it," Giancarlo corrected. "If you hadn't gotten that one kid to stop helping me, we would have all drowned. I think he nearly choked me."

"He was trying his best to help."

Without meaning to, they both started to laugh at the memory of the four rescuers and the one rescued. The shared relief at having faced down disaster coursed through them and made the memory comical. Beneath the blanket, Aleta felt Giancarlo take her hand in his. She shivered—from cold, no doubt.

Except the cold, from clingy damp clothes and a bodily remembrance of the frigid water, was broken where her body met his. Broken by a radiating heat.

His leg touched hers, his shoulder brushed against her own, their hips were joined in an effort to share the blanket issued by a distracted paramedic.

Boy Scouts learn that rubbing two dry sticks together causes a flame, but Aleta was beginning to think that two wet bodies could do the same. A tightening of her stomach, a trembling in her legs, a dizziness that she knew wasn't just the result of the excitement of the rescue—these were sensations she had never experienced. Had only read of. Had only dreamed of.

She had better watch herself, she knew.

The real Prince Giancarlo would be as easy to fall in love with as the imaginary, *International Snoop* Giancarlo had been.

After all, falling in love had happened to better women than she.

As he took her hand in his, she noted that he did not seem to suffer the same excitement as she. His hands were steady and warm, his grip confident and assured.

Of course his hands are steady, Aleta reminded herself. This man is experienced, a member of the jet set, a sophisticated...

"Excuse me, folks, my name is Ron Allen, and I'm from the *Chicago Daily*."

Aleta and Giancarlo looked up at the tall, heavyset man who stood before them, notebook in hand.

"The police said that you're the two who saved the three boys," Mr. Allen continued, with a note of boredom that was meant, no doubt, to communicate his world-weariness. "I just want to get your names for our story."

Aleta stared up at the reporter. She didn't dare tell him that this was the prince of Monticello.

"John Anderson," Giancarlo said calmly, as the reporter wrote in his notebook. "And this is my wife, Betty. That's short for Elizabeth."

Aleta's eyes widened as she listened to Giancarlo give the reporter an address. Amazingly, though, he named a street that was located in a blue-collar neighborhood in which a John and Betty Anderson might very well live.

"We were so happy we could help the boys," Giancarlo continued, looking over to Aleta briefly with a wink. "But it was nothing, really."

The reporter nodded, and continued writing.

"Hank! Could you get a picture of the Andersons here?" Ron shouted. He turned back to the couple. "Could you give us a big smile, folks?"

A couple of flashes erupted in Aleta's face as the photographer crouched in front of them and took a few shots.

"Mrs. Anderson, you have to smile," Mr. Allen scolded. "And you can't close your eyes, even if the flash hurts."

"I think my wife isn't up for pictures right now," Giancarlo said. "Maybe a better shot would be of one of the boy's mothers—what about that woman who just stepped out of the patrol car? She seems to be . . ."

As Ron Allen disappeared, the photographer stared at Giancarlo.

"There's something awfully familiar about your face," he said as he crouched nearer to the prince. "Do I know you or something?"

Aleta felt Giancarlo stiffen beside her. He silently shook his head, but his denial seemed to prod the photographer's memory.

"Hank! Would you get over here! I got the mother standing right here—she's ready for a shot!"

Hank hesitated at the sound of Ron Allen's voice but he wasn't dissuaded from searching Giancarlo's face and then Aleta's. Giancarlo looked away toward the horizon, avoiding the photographer's eyes.

"I know you from somewhere," Hank said, ignoring another shouted instruction from the reporter.

As he peered into Giancarlo's face, Aleta was certain that at any moment, he would know—and their pictures would be splattered all over the papers, her privacy would be shattered, the office would be crawling with...

"The bowling league!" she said suddenly. "You wouldn't happen to bowl at Fairlanes on Milwaukee Avenue, would you, Hank?"

Whatever thought had been forming in Hank's mind dissolved.

"No, no. I don't bowl."

"That's too bad. I thought you looked like one of the guys from the Red Demons teams. John here is the head of his team, the Blue Angels, and he..."

But Hank had fled, trotting over to a squad car for a candid shot of the relieved mother hugging her child.

"Thanks," Giancarlo said. "I thought that guy had really blown our cover."

"No, I think we fooled them."

Giancarlo threw off their blanket and motioned her to follow him. As they slipped away, Aleta let him take her hand easily in his.

"You're right," Giancarlo said. "I think we fooled them—" he paused "—Betty."

Aleta giggled and the look of understanding and sharing that passed between them opened her heart and made her forget the awkwardness of their circumstances.

"John," she said, following him away from the crowd.

Chapter Six

The prince and his newest gal pal, Aleta Clayton, would have remained incognito had it not been for the quick thinking of *Chicago Daily* photographer Hank Gordon, who recognized the modest prince even though His Highness had given their names to the press as John and Betty Anderson. The prince and Aleta are credited by police officers with saving the three unfortunate boys from drowning in the deadly waters of Lake Michigan.

"Those boys were goners," police officer Jackson Peters explained. "I always thought jet-setters were too snooty to save someone, but I was wrong. He dove right in and so did the girl. The prince deserves a medal. She does, too."

The *Snoop* agrees. Our reporters have long been aware of the prince's sensitive and heroic streak, which first evidenced itself two years ago when the prince saved another potential drowning victim on the chopping waters off the Monticello coast....

"You really must have been proud of yourself," Queen Marianya said in a voice which made quite clear that she didn't share those sentiments. She reached for the box of tissue-wrapped truffles near her chaise.

"Saving the boys was wonderful," she added, softening her tone. "And for that, I'm proud. It's the rest of it I could do without."

The *International Snoop* fell from her lap and, as it landed on the plush Aubusson rug, its lurid headline stared up at Giancarlo.

Her Hero? Chicago Gal Nabs Noble Beau.

He and Aleta had certainly fooled the press—but only for an instant, it seemed.

Beneath the headline was a grainy black-and-white photo of himself and Aleta, sharing their blanket on the cement steps overlooking the lake. His wet hair was slicked back while hers tumbled wildly about her face.

The accompanying caption highlighted the tearful sobs of the mother of one of the boys pledging her eternal gratitude to the prince and to all of Monticello.

The caption also included a questionable suggestion that under the blanket, Aleta and the prince were "more than the best of friends."

Giancarlo sighed and put his empty china cup and saucer on the marble occasional table by his chair. He stood up and walked to the window to avoid the piercing stare of his mother. And that of Hortensio, who, with his arms crossed in front of him, stood in the doorway that led to another of the many rooms in the penthouse suite of the Ambassador East Hotel.

"You must have thought you fooled the press," the queen continued, tiring of the truffles. She held the box out in Hortensio's direction. The diminutive aide leapt to the side of her Highness and discreetly disposed of the box. "This reflects very poorly on the future princess—because of the implication that her spotless demeanor is somehow...compromised. Giancarlo, you cannot be photographed beneath a blanket with that girl if she's to be the mother of the future heir."

Queen Marianya fixed the folds of her silk-and-chiffon dressing gown. Giancarlo turned to face her and when she looked up at him, she briefly held the countenance familiar to so many of her subjects.

She was the iron lady, who had married the reigning prince in an extravagant royal wedding that had ended the year 1958 on an elegant, reckless note. She had been a young slip of a girl, set loose like a newly formed butterfly from her family's shelter and she had soon developed a reputation for frivolity. Her face, permanently frozen in girlish laughter, had been on every magazine's society page. At Parisian fashion shows. At Monticellan festivals. At the Riviera.

Yet, barely two years later, she stood unsmiling at the graveside of her husband—he had crashed at Le Mans. For weeks, rumors abounded that Monticello's five-hundred-year run of good luck had ended, that under the terms of the 1456 treaty with Spain, the principality would be dissolved and its citizens returned to Spain. There was even the beginning of nationwide panic as Monticello citizens considered what would happen if they lost their autonomy to Spain. The Spanish, for their part, began to flex their long-dormant muscles as they considered the riches that would come with the tiny principality.

But then the palace announced, with enormous relief, that Marianya was pregnant with an heir to the throne. There was rejoicing in the streets, homes, schools and churches of Monticello—followed by intense and worried scrutiny of the pregnant, mournful queen. The pregnancy, thanks be to God, went well and a healthy son, Giancarlo, was born.

Queen Marianya had vowed that Monticello would never again come that close to destruction. She had ruled the principality with determination, changing quickly from an immature child to a woman. She had never remarried, had never even been linked by rumor and innuendo to any of the suitable men who visited Monticello's royal palace each year. She had devoted herself entirely to raising Monticello's last hope—her son. There had never been a romantic interest to her life, once her husband's casket was lowered into the ground. Thirty-three years before.

She had steered Monticello through a hundred crises, although she increasingly turned responsibilities over to Giancarlo, who seemed more adept at negotiating the increasingly complicated waters of economic and political stability.

And all she asked, as she never tired of telling Giancarlo, was that she could rest—could turn over her subjects and remaining duties to a prince with an heir already born.

As the eyes of mother and son met, the queen's expression softened. He had been the cause of so many sacrifices, of so many difficult choices—yet, a mother can never begrudge her child anything. And a mother never regrets the superhuman efforts that go into raising a child.

"Damn you, Giancarlo, I wanted to lecture you quite sternly." The Queen laughed, and patted an empty spot on the chaise. Giancarlo sat down near his mother. "You have to marry soon. I'm an old woman and my days are taken up entirely with this worry about grandchildren."

"Old woman?" Giancarlo chuckled. "You still turn heads, Mother."

Marianya shook her head, looking up briefly at Hortensio, whose face remained as impassive as it had throughout the morning.

Then the queen remembered that she had flown to Chicago this day to lecture her son, to prod him—not to let him sidetrack her with flattery.

"Giancarlo, you have to marry this girl—quickly, before the press catches the two of you beneath silk sheets," she said. "Or move on to another bride. Either way, you have to hurry."

"I've already asked Aleta to marry and she has said no."

Marianya's eyes opened wide with disbelief. There is no mother who believes that a woman can reject her son—but how much more true that is for a queen and a prince.

"She said no?"

Giancarlo shrugged, embarrassed by the definitiveness of his failure.

"Your Highness, if I could interrupt," Hortensio said, leaving his perch at the doorway to sit at one of the tables that were arranged about the chaise. "His Highness has indeed asked her and she has said no. But I believe the 'no' could mean 'yes' and most probably means 'maybe'."

"Oh, really?" Marianya pushed the sterling coffee-pot toward Hortensio and motioned an invitation to drink coffee with her. "Tell me more."

"Don't listen to him," Giancarlo commanded.

Hortensio shrugged and poured himself some coffee. Then he refilled the queen's cup in a manner so intimate that Giancarlo was momentarily caught off guard.

"The prince is—how shall I say—not very good at reading the language of women," the aide said, settling back into a feline slouch. "All he has ever had to read in a woman's eyes is yes, yes and yes. He has never read the hesitation of a woman's heart, never seen the moment when a woman is torn between the yes of her desires and the no of reason."

"Hortensio, you put it so movingly." Marianya sighed.

"Well, I believe I know a little about American women," he responded. "American women want to be wooed, want to be courted. Although I suppose every woman wants that. Don't you think, Your Highness?"

Giancarlo's anger erupted. "You talk about this marriage as if it were about love," he exclaimed, leaping to his feet to pace about the spacious sitting room. "This marriage has nothing to do with love! It's about a dynasty. It's about a country. It's about responsibility. It's about obligation. And it's an obligation that this American girl doesn't seem to understand she shares."

As if broken from a spell, Marianya resumed her famous stern expression, one seen repeatedly in magazines and newspapers throughout the world.

"You're absolutely right," she said with conviction. "If this girl is so foolish as to pass up a marriage which would take her from her dreary existence, and if she's determined to shirk her responsibility as a daughter of Monticello, you must move onto the next candidate— we simply must conclude this search for a wife immediately. All of Monticello rests on your shoulders."

Hortensio placed his cup back on the table.

"You are absolutely right, Your Highness," he said.

A maid quietly entered the room and informed the queen that her first appointment for the day was within the hour and what would Her Highness be wearing? Giancarlo gave a perfunctory kiss to his mother's cheek and returned to his rooms to read over his notes for a meeting with a group of businessmen. He was determined to put this morning's conversation behind him.

He was not very pleased when Hortensio followed him.

"You know, you're a pain in the...neck, sometimes, Hortensio," he said a little more forcefully than he meant to. "I'm sorry to hurt your feelings, and I'm sorry about ditching you yesterday—but I'm not sorry about anything else. I know what to do about women and I deeply resent the idea that you think you know Aleta better than I."

"Ah, but I do," Hortensio proclaimed softly. "You have spent so many years being so...good a catch, that you've never had to be a fisherman."

"Well, that...fish out there named Aleta isn't biting," Giancarlo said angrily. "She's holding out for love and all I can dangle in front of her is a crown and a lifetime of obligation. She won't take it and I can't blame her. If I had the choice, there's some days that I wouldn't be who I am, either."

Hortensio shook his head.

"My dear, naive prince."

"What do you mean?" Giancarlo asked with suspicion.

"You are so naive. If you asked her today, if you gave her your ring, she would say yes."

"Like hell she would," Giancarlo said, but then he hesitated. "She would still say no. She said no once, and she'd say it again. She wants love. She wants eternal, unqualified love—and a crown, a palace and a title won't change her mind."

Hortensio shrugged.

"I stand corrected," he said, in a manner that made very clear that he wasn't corrected in the slightest.

Giancarlo felt like slamming his fist into the wall—Hortensio was so aggravating!

Instead, Giancarlo gathered up the papers he needed for his meeting and searched aimlessly through the room for his tie.

"Is this the one you wish to wear?" Hortensio said, holding up a blue and yellow striped silk tie.

"Yes, it is." Giancarlo grabbed the tie from his aide's hand, and immediately regretted the way that his anger was affecting him.

She would refuse him, wouldn't she?

It was almost a point of pride to him that she would, that she wouldn't say yes to the things he had to offer, to the things that any other woman in the world would kill for.

She wanted him—and the other women wanted only what he represented.

But since Aleta knew that he didn't want to be married, had absolutely no interest in being married, wasn't rushing into marriage like some lovesick boy—she would say no.

He smiled as he thought of his admiration for her.

For her determination to have a marriage based on love. What a simple, yet deceptively complicated, requirement. And it was one that she had had the courage and the integrity to hold on to, even when another woman might have made another choice.

It wasn't the only thing he had to admire about her, he admitted, as his ruminations turned to her hair that tousled so out of control. And to her golden brown eyes that sparkled with joy and delight at the simplest of pleasures. And to the curves that seemed boyish at times—but when she had emerged from the lake with her clothes clinging, those curves had reminded him quite clearly that she was a woman.

A woman ready to give her love to a man.

Even if she didn't know it. Even if she was too innocent to realize the profound intimacy that she would share. With a man.

He could imagine that any other woman he had known wouldn't have been content to hold his hand, as she had done beneath the blanket and later, as he had walked her to her home. Any other woman would have been determined to seduce him, to conquer the prince, to stake out her feminine worth with his embrace.

And yet, that quiet moment of holding hands had meant so much more to him than a dozen more explicit gestures.

No, she would never say yes.

At least she wouldn't today.

And he didn't have the time to woo her the way that she wanted, the way that she deserved, to be wooed— even if he had the innate desire to court. His obligations to the well-being of his country were crystal clear. An heir must be produced. A marriage must be settled. Three million people who felt as strongly about Spain as their forefathers had five centuries before were depending on him.

It was enough to make any man wary of the institution of marriage.

Hortensio followed the prince as he strode to the elevator and both men were quiet as they glided to the first floor.

The lobby was strangely empty, free of the reporters and photographers who had been trailing the prince for his stay.

"Where are our shadows?" the prince asked. He led Hortensio through the revolving doors to the waiting car.

"They are following the queen," Hortensio said, as they settled into the back seat. "Apparently, her appearance at Marshall Field's to promote Monticellan designers is much more newsworthy than anything you shall do today."

"I'm very glad of that," Giancarlo said, and pulled out his notes for the coming meeting. One thing he was grateful for was that his mother was always so much more interesting to the press—naturally friendly to the herds that followed her, she was Monticello's best public relations tool.

Certainly making up for her "bad boy" son.

He studied the notes for his meeting. The work he did wasn't the stuff of photo opportunities, but it was much more important. And relentlessly demanding.

The graphs and charts and analysis setting forth reasons why smart American businessmen should be investing in Monticello swam in front of him. These tools would help him persuade the group assembled this morning that Monticello was worthy of their interest.

He couldn't concentrate.

Foreign investors on average netted eighteen percent per annum on investments in Monticello real estate while American investors did better because of their ability to take advantage of recent Internal Revenue Service rulings on corporate taxation of...

Giancarlo looked out the window at the buildings of the city. He couldn't get her out of his head. And he couldn't get Hortensio's insidious comments out of his head, either.

He looked back, determined to concentrate on his papers. Concentrate, he commanded himself.

While investments in other European properties netted fourteen percent per annum, Monticello...

"What are you looking at?" he said, without looking up from his notes.

Hortensio shook his head.

"Your Highness, I'm not looking at anything," he protested. "Absolutely nothing."

"You were too looking at me," Giancarlo contended, irritated with his aide and with his own inability to maintain control over the situation. But when had he ever had control since he had met Aleta? "Hortensio, I command you to stop looking at me like that."

With a sullen, exaggerated turn of his jaw, Hortensio looked out the window.

"I'm sorry," Giancarlo apologized, tired of his aide's petulance. "I'm in a bad mood. I'm preoccupied."

"Of course, Your Highness."

"With this...stuff," Giancarlo explained, waving the papers.

Hortensio didn't move.

"Of course, Your Highness."

"All right, dammit, you can look at me!"

Hortensio's shoulders relaxed and he smiled at his charge.

"I'm very concerned about this meeting," Giancarlo continued. "It means a lot to our country."

"Of course, Your Highness."

They drove in silence. Giancarlo continued to struggle with his work.

Under Monticello law, foreign investors must register with the Ministry of...

"All right, dammit, let's drive to her office!" Giancarlo exclaimed, flinging down his notes. "But I'm telling you, she's going to say no."

Hortensio smiled broadly, and then, when he saw the scowl on his Prince's face, stifled his excitement. He quickly instructed the driver on the route to the McCormick building.

"She'll say no," Giancarlo repeated. "She'll tell me no, and, frankly, that's what I admire about her. She stands by her principles. She wants love in her marriage and she won't settle for anything else."

"Of course, Your Highness."

"If I had time I could court her, could woo her, and for the first time in my life, I would know a woman who loved me and not just my throne. *If* I wanted to get married, and that is, of course, a big *if*."

"Of course, Your Highness."

"Hortensio, you have no idea what it's like to know that your power over women is just because of what you represent and not who you are. And you have no idea what it is to be forced into a marriage."

Hortensio nodded, well aware of the doubts within Giancarlo's life, doubts that had remained subconscious before this trip to Chicago.

"Hortensio, I have a duty. And I'll discharge it. Don't worry," he added, holding up his hand against Hortensio's unspoken protests. "I know my country depends on me. After this morning, we'll go back to our list. There is a queen for Monticello out there. But it's not Aleta."

"As you wish, Your Highness."

"It's not how I wish at all," Giancarlo said sadly.

As the limousine glided to a stop, Hortensio removed his seat belt.

"No, Hortensio, I'm doing this by myself," Giancarlo ordered. "But I think you better call ahead to the meeting and tell them I'll be late. And you'd better cancel my appointments for this evening and tomorrow. I'd like to leave Chicago this afternoon."

"But, Your Highness, the Monticello consulate is holding its welcoming dinner for you this evening," Hortensio protested. "And tomorrow morning, there's the breakfast with the Chamber of Commerce!"

"Well, my mother can go to both events," Giancarlo said grimly. "God, I hate this city."

But it wasn't the city that he hated—it was the disappointment that would always be associated with it.

The disappointment of growing up and knowing that duty would always take first place. When he had been a young child and had realized what being a prince meant, he had delighted in the petty ordering of servants and the dreams of royal commands for dessert for breakfast that he planned for his adult reign.

Instead, he had discovered responsibility. Responsibility so enormous that it engulfed his life.

Chicago wasn't the city he hated.

It was a city he loved, in spite of how he knew his relationship with Aleta would end. The sunshine that so quickly could change to gusty gray. Sid and Estelle's deli. The lake. The long walks. Her hand placed shyly in his.

Chicago was his city.

And Aleta's.

But a city that would always remind him of the obligations he couldn't shirk. Millions of people depended on him, depended on the sacrifice he was about to make.

Tired of waiting for the elevator, he raced up the eight flights—taking two steps at a time. He felt his adrenaline coursing through him, felt it wash away, but not erase, the terrible sadness he knew was coming.

He would never see her again. He knew she would refuse him. Refuse him unless he was able to gain her hand as any commoner would.

But he also knew that the press of time, the press of the need for an heir, hunted him down—he couldn't waste months on the pursuit of his bride.

And, of course, Aleta would never settle for being a royal mistress.

And those very facts made him love her, love her as he would never love a woman who would look at a royal marriage as a way of escaping a dull and dreary life.

He yanked open the smoked-glass door of McCormick, and startled the receptionist as he strode past her toward Aleta's office. When he reached the tiny room, four women looked up at him—wide-eyed and openmouthed with surprise.

But there was only one woman he was interested in.

Aleta stood up from behind her desk, and he grabbed her hand.

"Come here," he commanded brusquely. "I have to talk to you."

Looking as frightened as a dove by his order, she obediently followed him to the hallway and he breathed deeply of her perfume, a gentle mix of lily of the valley and talc. As he tried to gather his thoughts, he somehow knew that the scent of her would follow him, would remind him always of these few days. She looked up at him, half-fearful and half-baffled.

Oh, Aleta, I love you—yes, dammit—I love you.

But I love you for the very fact that you have the courage to refuse me.

He started to speak, to ask the question that his mother, his aide, his whole country wanted asked.

And answered.

Then he noticed three pairs of curious eyes peering at him from the office. Maggie, Rhoda and Carla.

"Is anything wrong?" Maggie asked. "Is there something we can help with?"

He shook his head and, claiming Aleta's hand, led her into the next office. Spacious, with a view of the lake, it was a perfect place for the goodbyes they were about to say.

Except there was a portly man seated at the desk, who looked surprised and angry at the interruption.

"What are you doing barging into my office?"

"You must leave," Giancarlo said.

"But this is my office! Who the hell are you to..."

"And I'm commanding you to leave."

"Mr. McCormick, he's a prince," Maggie explained, racing into the office. "You had better do what he says."

Still complaining, Mr. McCormick allowed himself to be led from the office, and Maggie closed the door behind them.

Not before giving an excited smile and a thumbs-up signal to Aleta.

Leading her to the window, Giancarlo again organized his thoughts—putting together his words in the way he had so often for impromptu talks to thousands. There was so much he wanted to say, so much he wanted to explain, to this very special woman.

Except . . . how did Hortensio put it?

He had never been a fisherman.

"Aleta, look out the window," he started. "Look at the lake, at the buildings, at the skyline, at all the people down there."

She did as as she was told, staring out at the panoramic view as if she wanted very much to share in whatever he was searching for. Out there. In the freedom of the wide-open sky.

"You'd have to give up everything," he continued. "You'd have to give up everything that is part of your life. Everything you know, everything you do. Pop Tarts. Diet Coke. Your friends."

"Yes?" she asked, turning toward him.

He took a deep breath. Why did she have to be so damned beautiful when he had to ask her? And she had to refuse?

"Aleta, will you marry me?" he said finally, turning away from her. He was surprised by the pain that came with each of the four simple words.

"Yes, Giancarlo, I will."

Chapter Seven

Something was wrong.

Very wrong.

Moonlight and roses, soft music and champagne—if Aleta could have chosen the most romantic setting for the moment she said yes to marriage, it wouldn't have been in Mr. McCormick's office on a Thursday morning.

But any atmosphere can be romantic if two people are in love. And every wife remembers the moment she said yes as being suffused with a special glow.

It's not the atmosphere that's wrong, Aleta thought, as she felt an icy chill gather within Mr. McCormick's office. Her words, her excited yes, had caused the change.

She expected to be gathered up into his arms, into an embrace that would seal their eternal commitment. But when she answered his heartfelt plea, she was almost certain his eyes had grown cold and cloudy. He had—

there was no doubt—turned away from her, however briefly, staring at the lake as if entranced.

She had said yes because she meant it, because the day before—a Wednesday as much the middle of the week as any other ordinary Wednesday—that special day had convinced her that she could see within the arrogance and aloofness to a man so much more wonderful than her distant prince.

His hesitation was only for a second, a momentary lapse that to any other eyes would have been meaningless. When he turned back from his study of the lake, he was hers again—but with an essential part of him forever closed off from her, frozen and inaccessible.

No other woman would have noticed that moment. To Aleta, that instant of candor meant everything.

What had she done, except given in to the love that had exploded within her yesterday? She had been with him for a full and transforming day, with Giancarlo the man and not merely Giancarlo the prince.

Two very different men.

And she had fallen in love with the man she had talked with, she had held hands with, she had played hooky from her job with.

She was in love with him—and the love was so much more full than the from-a-distance crush that had carried her from *Snoop* issue to issue.

What had she done except give in—to love?

"Well, I guess that settles it," Giancarlo said at last, clapping his hands together in a forced joviality that Aleta knew neither of them felt. "My mother is in town—this evening's reception at the Monticello consulate would be an appropriate time to make the announcement."

"Of course," Aleta said woodenly. She slumped into an armchair in front of McCormick's desk.

"The evening will be rather formal," Giancarlo continued. "I'll send someone out to purchase some... appropriate clothes. The car will arrive to pick you up from here at five o'clock. You will change into your gown at the consulate. The queen always wears black at these occasions—you will probably be attired in a pastel."

She looked up at him, hoping for some crumb of warmth, some moment of understanding. Anything— a touch of his hand, a brief kiss, even a smile would allay her fears that somehow she had angered him, angered him by her very acceptance of him.

Who was this man she would call her husband? What had happened to the man who had eaten hot dogs from a truck the day before? What had happened to the man who had listened so intently to her description of her ordinary days—and who had made them seem exciting and worthwhile? What had happened to the man who had leapt into the water without a thought to his own safety? What had happened to the man who had ended the day at her doorstep with a kiss to the back of her hand that meant more to her than any of the groping kisses that previous dates had tried?

"You're going to make a wonderful princess," he continued, with a smile that didn't quite clear the cloudiness of his eyes. "I am so pleased that you will be my wife," he added, in a voice that could have just as easily been congratulating a Monticellan farmer on his crops or an international investor on his choice of the principality's banks as a resting place for his cash.

He knelt at her side. She thought he would take her into his arms, would kiss her the way that he had kissed so many women, would embrace her and share the joy that should come with a promise to marry.

"How about a kiss?"

"Yeah, we want to see the happy lovebirds!"

"Too bad we don't have champagne!"

The boisterous interruption from Maggie and the other women of the office, like a crew of circus performers barging in on a funeral, startled both Aleta and Giancarlo. The couple looked uncomfortably at the women, carefully avoiding being the first to give in to a kiss from the other.

While Maggie begged them to seal their engagement with an embrace, Rhoda and Carla frankly oohed and aahed their best wishes and I-told-you so's. Even Mr. McCormick managed a gruff congratulations as he came in and extended his hand to Giancarlo for a gentlemanly shake.

"I guess this means you won't be working here anymore," McCormick said to Aleta, patting her on the back with exaggerated joviality. "I guess you'll be too busy with the jet set to deal with McCormick's monthly bills."

"I was listening at the keyhole," Maggie explained in a rapid rush of words. "I hope you don't mind, Your Majesty, but I feel a certain responsibility toward Aleta and I just wanted to make sure..."

"Oh, how wonderful this all is!" Carla interrupted. "I'm going to be able to tell my grandkids about how I was a part of history. I was there when Aleta and the prince got engaged!"

"It's so romantic," Rhoda added, dabbing her eyes with a tissue. "Isn't it wonderful to be in love?"

No, it's horrible to be in love, Aleta wanted to shout. *Horrible when you have no idea what terrible thoughts are in the mind of the man you love.*

He had said everything he was supposed to say. He had done everything a lover should. He had asked her to marry him and she had said yes. What could be simpler?

Yet, where was the confidence that this commitment should give her? Why did she doubt so much, at this— a moment that should be filled with the certainty of marriage?

When their eyes met, as he stood and pulled her into his arms for the much-requested kiss that would seal their love, there was no flicker of recognition that she was the woman he loved, no sparkle of joy, no silent promise of undying devotion.

Was she imagining things?

Or was he just overwhelmed by the enormity of what he had asked and what she had answered?

She remembered that when Carla's husband had asked her to marry him and Carla had said yes, he became so unnerved that he kissed his mother and shook his new fiancée's hand.

She let him take her hand in his—so cold his were, so lifeless even as they gripped her own. *Stop having expectations about how a future husband should act,* she commanded herself.

After all, he's just nervous.

Giancarlo reached down and kissed her as the onlookers sighed. Except, perhaps for Mr. McCormick, who wondered aloud if he was ever getting his office back.

The kiss, which could have reassured her, did nothing to lessen her unease. A bittersweet brush of his lips against hers, as awkward as the few kisses she had endured on high school dates.

And then, abruptly, he released her.

The excited chattering of her office mates resumed.

"I have to leave," he said quietly.

"Duty calls?" Aleta asked, surprised at the note of bitterness that had crept into her voice.

If he noticed anything amiss, he was expert at hiding it.

"A meeting with bank officials," he explained. "I shall see you this evening."

With a final dismal kiss on her cheek, he was gone.

Aleta's arms felt awkward and gangly with no beloved to hold—she had never noticed the absence of love in her life as acutely as at this moment. She slumped back into the armchair across from McCormick's desk.

"It's so exciting!" Rhoda exclaimed. "Will you two have the wedding in Monticello?"

"Of course, silly," Maggie answered. "Do you think that Monticello royalty is going to marry at a Las Vegas chapel?"

"Have you had a chance to meet the queen?" Carla asked. "Omigosh, I just realized we gotta give you a shower."

"At my wedding shower, I got more guest towels than I could use if my house were a hotel," Rhoda said. "I don't think we can give her the usual kind—she's not going to need sheets or colanders or new pots and pans at the castle. They got all that stuff, I'm sure."

"I guess you're right," Carla conceded.

"But we have to give her a shower of some sort," Maggie said. "It just wouldn't be right not to. Now what can we do?"

"How about leaving my office?" Mr. McCormick barked. He had sat down at his desk and was reviewing the papers spread before him.

"All right, all right," Maggie exclaimed. "Come on, girls, we'd better go back to ours—we can spend the whole afternoon thinking about the wedding on company time."

Mr. McCormick growled, but his exaggerated manner made clear that he understood that wedding work certainly took precedence over bookkeeping.

Carla, Rhoda and Maggie walked into the hallway, chattering a mile a minute about weddings, showers, royalty and the "to-die-for" prince.

Aleta struggled to get the energy to follow.

"I guess this means I have to give you my two-week notice," she said dismally. If anyone had told her that she wouldn't be jumping for joy when she finally had this conversation with Mr. McCormick, she would have told them they were crazy.

But that was before she said yes to a marriage to the prince. The monthly figures and the camaraderie of her office, the daily routine were sounding so much more comforting.

"Yeah, I figured that you'd be leaving," McCormick said, without looking up. "I'll miss you—you were my best bookkeeper. If I get somebody half as good as you, I'll consider myself lucky."

"But, Mr. McCormick, you're always yelling at me," Aleta said, utterly surprised at his comment. "I thought you hated my work and that you think I'm lazy and slow and incompetent. At least that's what you've said."

"The woman you replaced took longer and longer to finish each month's invoices," he said, chuckling at the memory. "The day I realized I was holding in my hand invoices for July and it was snowing outside was her last day on the job. You always have them ready on time, or at least within a few hours."

"So how come you're always yelling at me?"

He shrugged as if she were asking one of the imponderable questions that had been plaguing mankind for centuries.

"Maybe 'cause you never fight back. You know, I'm not an ogre. I'm not a bogeyman. But my temper gets the better of me sometimes—and you've never figured out that I can take it just as well as I can dish it out. The others yell back at me and you know what? I've never fired any of them. Or even thought worse of them for it."

As he returned to his papers, Aleta thought about his reply. Had she really misjudged him? Should she have stood up for herself—dished it right back at him whenever he threw a tantrum? Were her office mates right when they told her that she should stand up for herself?

But there hadn't been much fight left in her when her mother had died.

Or maybe Mom devoted so much of her life to you, a voice in her head cautioned, *devoted so much of her life to fighting your battles for you that you never learned to do anything for yourself.*

After all, her mother had raised her to be a princess.

Perhaps she had even been brought up more like spoiled royalty than Giancarlo himself. The only difference being that, in her, the worst trait of being a princess was that she didn't have much of a spine.

"You know, for having just snagged the man of your dreams, you don't look so happy." Mr. McCormick interrupted her thoughts. "I mean, when I think of all the hours I've paid your wages to have you moon over articles and pictures chronicling his every waking instant..."

"You're wrong, Mr. McCormick," Aleta said defensively, rising to her feet. She wanted to run and hide, to dissolve into sobs. But she was royalty now—or almost royalty. "You're wrong, Mr. McCormick. I'm very happy. I'm ecstatic over my wedding."

"Coulda fooled me."

His words echoed in her ears as she walked down the hallway to her office.

"More tea, Miss Clayton?"

"No, thank you, Your Highness," Aleta answered, staring into her empty cup. She looked up at Giancarlo, hoping for some encouragement. But he was signing some documents at the Queen Anne desk by the window. Hortensio stood at his side, pointing out the places where the prince's signature was necessary. "And you should call me Aleta," she added, not sure whether one told a queen what to do.

"Well, Aleta, I'm very pleased that you arrived early for the reception so that we could have this chance to get to know one another," the queen said, putting her cup down on the lacquered side table. "But I simply must return to the consulate dressing room to prepare for the evening. It's been wonderful to have this chat."

"Yes, it has," Aleta said mechanically, rising as she now knew she was supposed to when the queen exited a room.

Alone again, she sat back down and smoothed the pale yellow organza skirt of the dress that had arrived at the McCormick offices with the limousine at five o'clock. She had ridden alone to the consulate and had been shown by a secretary to her dressing room. A maid had helped her with the delicate pearl buttons that went up the back of the dress, and had carefully arranged Aleta's hair into a smooth and simple chignon.

There had been a jewelry box among the accessories given her. Inside was her engagement ring—a sapphire and three diamonds that she remembered from an *International Snoop* article the year before on the Monticello royal jewels.

It was the ring that the first princess of Monticello had worn in 1456—it was a gift to show the loyalty the five knights who had fought to defend her land felt for her, as if leading the battle against the Spanish weren't enough.

She had wondered briefly if she was supposed to wait for the prince to place it on her finger—after all, the ring was supposed to be a declaration of his love for her.

She ended up putting it on herself when she was told by a maid that the prince would not be arriving at the consulate until it was nearly time for the reception.

Then, with the unfamiliar weight upon her hand, Aleta had been led to this sitting room to meet the queen.

Giancarlo had arrived moments later, giving Aleta a kiss on the cheek and then giving his mother a similar one. Pleading commitments of work, he had immediately sat at the opulent desk and signed the numerous royal proclamations thanking various Chicago businessmen and community leaders for their help to Monticello.

And now, with the only sound in the room being the scratching of his pen against the linen paper, Aleta felt more alone than she had ever in her life. She was engaged. To the man she loved. To the most eligible man in the world. She had a ring that sparkled and, if the light was just right, threw rainbows onto nearby surfaces. And yet...

The scratching stopped. Aleta looked up to see Giancarlo snapping the cap back on to the expensive fountain pen.

"That will be all, Hortensio," he said crisply, clearly not tortured by the doubts and misgivings that Aleta had wrestled with throughout the afternoon. "Find me a list of guests for this evening for my review."

"Of course, Your Highness."

With a bow, Hortensio was gone.

And Aleta was alone with her prince.

He stood in front of her, arm outstretched. For a brief moment, she hesitated—remembering the way that her mind had replayed his hesitation, his sudden chill, as she accepted with joy his offer of marriage. The obsessive remembrance had been particularly painful while she had been consigned to an office with her friends—friends who babbled excitedly all afternoon about the coming wedding.

But he was, after all, the man she loved. Had always loved. Would always...

She leapt up to his arms, thinking that he would bring her into an embrace that the afternoon's lack of privacy had deterred.

Instead, he held her somewhat apart from himself.

"We are to dance this evening," he explained. "There will be many observers from the press, particularly since we shall announce our engagement before the orchestra arrives. We will want to move well together. Do you waltz?"

She shook her head.

"Then I must teach you," he said.

Within seconds, he had swept her across the floor and Aleta found herself desperately concentrating on making her feet follow his as they glided about the spacious sitting room. Giancarlo gracefully negotiated through paths of furniture and glided to the rhythm that he set.

"Two-two-three-four, three-two-three-four," he chanted as Aleta's feet kept up with his. "You're doing great. Now let's quicken the rhythm a little. Four-two-three-four..."

He was tantalizingly close, his mouth at her ear, one hand at the small of her back, the other lightly clasping her right hand. She could smell the light mix of talc and citrus emanating from his skin. She could feel the roughness of a late-afternoon shadow on his jaw as it brushed against her forehead. And the press of his muscular thigh against her own—did her leg tremble or was it merely the rustling of the unfamiliarly lush fabric of her skirt?

She was tempted by the intimacy that eluded her. She wanted a fuller embrace. She wanted...something that her youth—or was it inexperience?—didn't even allow her to understand. She couldn't lead him, she couldn't take from him, when she knew so little about what exactly she would give and receive in such a moment.

"Giancarlo," she whispered, as he continued to count, as he continued to dance her across the room. She took a deep breath. "Giancarlo, I thought this afternoon that you were angry at me for having said yes. For having said that I would marry you."

At first she thought he hadn't heard her. There was no change in the rhythm of his feet, no change in his chant.

"Giancarlo," she whispered again, wondering at the fear that had crept into her voice.

Giancarlo stopped dancing, abruptly coming to a halt. If he wanted to pull away from her, Aleta wouldn't have let him. She clung to his arms. She wanted him now, wanted his reassurance.

"Why did you think that?" he asked.

Aleta's heart felt as if it had leapt into her throat.

He hadn't said no. He hadn't laughed at how silly she was being and kissed away her doubts. He hadn't denied anything.

"Because you don't seem all that happy for a groom," she said at last, unable to fully articulate the doubts within her.

His jaw pulsed with tension and his mouth set into a determined line.

"But why did you say 'yes' when I asked you to marry me?" he asked. "Why did you change your mind from the first time I asked, when you said no?"

"Because I love you," Aleta explained. She saw a flicker of disbelief cross his face. "I love you," she repeated with more force. "Why did you ask me?"

How could he explain himself, how could he explain the complicated forces that had brought him to her office? He loved her, he had decided. And yet, his question, his proposal—meant in love—had only been a test. A test of love that she had failed. That any woman would have failed.

He knew now that it was wrong. It had been wrong to appear in her office and ask her the most important question a man can ever ask a woman when his love for her depended on her refusal. Especially, he thought to himself as he studied her eyes, especially when she was still so young and innocent.

And yet, was she truly innocent?

When she said she loved him, he could not help but think of the women who had said those very words before. Said those words with the hope that such a love would be returned, returned complete with a palace, throne and crown.

"Why did you ask me again to marry?" Aleta repeated.

He stumbled with his words, for the first time in his life stripped of the smooth, graceful way with words that had served a prince well.

"I asked you... because..." He couldn't finish; he was unable to bring himself to explain how her reply had shocked him, had jolted him, had forcibly wrenched from within him his most private fears. And yet, her intense stare made clear that he would have to answer her.

If not now, soon.

He was relieved that the door to the sitting room opened—his mother swept into the room with Hortensio behind her.

"Should we go downstairs?" she asked with enthusiasm. The look of pride and happiness that she gave to the young couple reminded Giancarlo that the moment his mother had looked forward to for years was within minutes. She wanted to give up more and more of the responsibilities of the throne and this evening would mark the beginning of that process.

She deserved it—deserved to be able to relax after thirty-odd years of service to her country. Service that had effectively cut off a life that a woman would want, a life that would have the love of a man as one of its parts.

And now, many of her ceremonial responsibilities could be turned over to the woman in his arms. And the queen, released, could seek new joys.

He looked at Aleta, wondering if this marriage would be everything she hoped for. Wondering what her real motivation had been. Wondering where the woman he had known yesterday had gone.

Not that it mattered.

There was no more time in his life now for high jinks, such as yesterday's. Every part of his life was now swallowed up by obligation to country.

Even his personal life. As thoroughly as his mother's life had been eaten up with obligation.

"We're ready," he said, drawing his mother's arm into the crook of his right arm and pulling Aleta to his left side. He carefully avoided looking into Aleta's eyes, knowing as he did that she had been more frightened than reassured by his inability to answer her direct question.

The trio followed Hortensio down the broad winding staircase into an elegant hallway. They stood in the doorway to the reception room, waiting while Hortensio slipped inside.

The prince felt the pressure of the two women at his side. One, filled with happiness at the marriage of her son. A second filled with anxiety about the coming party—that he could tell from the pressure of her fingers against his arm. If Hortensio didn't hurry, she'd draw blood.

But Giancarlo wondered about her true feelings about this marriage. The declaration of love didn't seem quite real—he wondered . . . and then he knew it didn't matter.

Duty was first and foremost.

The reception room doors swung open and within, a crowd of richly dressed guests stared with frank and open admiration at the royal visitors. Hortensio positioned himself at the side of the entranceway.

"Her Royal Highness, Queen Marianya of Monticello," Hortensio announced as guests began to dip in curtsies and bows. "His Highness, Prince Giancarlo and his betrothed." A rustle of excitement swept through the room. "His betrothed, Miss Aleta Maria Coronado Clayton of Chicago, Illinois."

As irrevocable as any wedding vows, the announcement of their betrothal bound them, Giancarlo knew. He held his head high, squeezed Aleta's arm to give her confidence and led the women into the crowd of excited guests.

Chapter Eight

"It says here that you had to go to a special doctor so that your virginity could be substantiated," Maggie said, pondering the accompanying photos in the *International Snoop*. "That's amazing. They could have just asked me. After all, you would have told me if there had been anybody, wouldn't you?"

"Of course, Maggie," Aleta said, carefully peeking out at the street from behind the lace curtains of her bedroom window. Her quiet neighborhood had been transformed into a carnival—complete with several minivans from local television stations, a crowd of photographers and reporters and a boisterous crowd of curious onlookers.

After loudly slurping the rest of her Diet Coke, Maggie successfully lobbed the can into the wastebasket beside Aleta's desk. Lounging on Aleta's bed for the past hour, she had kept her friend posted on all the details of her romance with the prince—at least, all the details as reported by the six magazines and newspapers she had bought at the White Hen on her way over to Aleta's apartment.

Aleta had called her when she woke up, when she realized that the crowd posted outside her home wasn't going to leave—and when she realized that this morning she didn't have the stomach to face them, as she would have to, in order to get to the bus stop.

And to wait in that mob for the morning bus to take her to the McCormick offices?

Utterly impossible.

"Wow! It says here you're descended from Señor Roberto Coronado, who saved Princess Gratanzia in 1456 from a band of marauding Spaniards."

"That's nice," Aleta replied dispiritedly. She pushed the curtains back into place and stepped away from the window.

"The *International Snoop* says you're to be admired for being self-supporting," Maggie continued. "And for working even if you are descended from such dizzying heights. Gee, Aleta, I feel so honored that you've been my friend all these years."

"Think nothing of it."

"Aleta! You know, you're going to have to face them sometime," Maggie said, letting the stack of publications slide to the floor. "I mean, you can't stay in here forever—stuck in this room, a prisoner."

"I just can't face them. They look so scary."

Maggie joined her at the window. The two women stared at the front lawn, careful to not get too close to the window. Aleta had already caused a stir with one such mistake and tomorrow, most likely, there would be photos of herself peering from that very window in every publication in the world. She didn't need to make it two pictures.

"You're right," Maggie confessed. "I don't think I could go out there, either. You're like a princess trapped in a tower—you need somebody to rescue you."

"I need a prince," Aleta whispered.

Maggie shrugged, the allusion to Giancarlo barely provoking any response. In the week since the announcement of Aleta's engagement, Maggie's profound interest in every detail of the prince's life had definitely faded.

He was, after all, a man just like any other—wasn't he?

"As long as you're going to be running off to Monticello to get married, do you mind if I borrow that purple sweater I really like?"

"Yeah, sure," Aleta answered, dropping down onto the bed with a heavy sigh. "It's somewhere in the closet."

"Don't worry, I'll find it."

While Maggie went through her clothes, finding every minute a few more things that she wanted to "borrow," Aleta woodenly thought of the ways that her life had changed since her engagement was announced.

She couldn't leave her house without a hundred people wanting her autograph, her picture, a few comments about this or that trivial issue. Strangers handed her flowers, boxes of candies and called out their well wishes—all of which only succeeded in embarrassing her. Her every move was reported—when, two evenings ago, she had used the wrong fork at a dinner hosted by the governor of Illinois, it was duly noted by the press.

And, worst of all, instead of relaxing with a pint of double chocolate-chip ice cream and a romance novel at the end of the day, each evening she had had to eat paprika-sprinkled chicken and Grand Marnier soufflés, and listen to boring speeches with hundreds of other people who... well, who stared at her.

As for her job with McCormick, it wasn't as if she loved her job so much that leaving it was the problem. After all, she would hardly have wanted to work in the bookkeeping department of McCormick for the rest of her life. It's just that, while listening to the chatter of her friends and going through the usual paperwork, she realized sadly that these familiar parts of her life were soon to be gone.

Replaced, presumably, by a loving marriage.

But even thoughts of her upcoming wedding didn't relieve her quiet sense of something gone wrong.

Or maybe it was precisely those thoughts of her upcoming wedding that disturbed her.

Oh, he was handsome. And attentive. And courteous. And he did everything in his power—and a considerable amount of power it was—to make her feel wonderful.

And sometimes she awoke in the middle of the night and wondered at the turn of events that had made her lifelong dream come true. Just as her mother had predicted.

But perhaps less romantically than her mother or she had anticipated.

They hadn't had a moment alone since their engagement was announced. No quiet dinners. No private breakfasts. No stolen embraces. All she had to show for her love was a chaste good-night kiss before the limousine drove her to her apartment building, now guarded by a security detail trained in Monticello.

Her engagement had all the earmarks of a merger, a treaty, a bargain between countries and customs and laws.

And not many of a love affair.

The press agreed that she was perfect: so gracious and charming, the tabloids declared. In the past week, she had been called regal, witty, demure and refreshing by people she didn't even know. Those were the nice things people said.

The bad thing was when she had read that she was "perfect wife material." Several magazines had picked up on the theme, carefully sounding neutral even as they strongly implied that the prince was using her for a dynastic solution to his troubles—a solution that would still allow him the company of more "risqué" companions while satisfying the letter of the requirements of Monticello's treaty with Spain and the principality's customs.

The articles fueled Aleta's already beleaguered imagination.

Wife material.

The fears that had for a single day disappeared had come back with a vengeance.

Was she deluding herself that they had ever been close, even on that one magical day? Would they find time for themselves during the planned honeymoon and goodwill tour of Australia? Or would they spend the rest of their lives on an endless receiving line, making thirty seconds of small talk with each person presented to them? Would she suffer through the coming years the humiliation of his not-so-private affairs?

A knock on the door startled Aleta and brought Maggie out from within the closet.

"Oh, God, the outside door to the building is supposed to be locked," Aleta said. "And there's a security guard to make sure that no one got in."

"He was there when I came," Maggie reassured her.

"So who is that?" Aleta begged, suddenly terrified that one of the reporters on the lawn had managed to slip past her defenses.

"Let me handle it," Maggie ordered. She stood at the door. "Who's there?"

"I happen to be the crown prince of Monticello."

Aleta raced to the door and flung it open. She threw herself into his arms, breathing in the woodsy smell, the security of him, the protectiveness that she needed so desperately. She clung to him as if she were drowning, drowning in self-doubt, fear and anxiety.

He hesitated a moment, his arms held apart from himself, apart from her, while he grappled with his own worries. He had been feeling the tightening noose of obligations in the past week and the sensation hadn't made him the most gracious of lovers.

But Giancarlo was, above all, an empathetic man and he understood the overwhelming events of the past few days all too well. How much worse it must be for a commoner—a woman who was used to dealing with her life in privacy.

"I tried calling you, but your phone had been unplugged," he said softly.

"I got so tired of the incessant calling from reporters!" she wailed. "I couldn't pick up the phone, I couldn't even go downstairs to pick up my mail."

"*Querida, querida,*" he muttered into her sweet-smelling hair. "This is becoming too much for you."

She curled farther within his comforting embrace.

"Darling, can't we go away?" she begged, lifting her head up. "Can't we escape like we did that one afternoon last week?"

He touched his finger to her cheek, gently wiping away the wet shadow of a tear that betrayed the depth of her emotions. Then he seemed to remember himself, remembered the part of himself that was, first and foremost, a prince.

"You don't understand what you've gotten yourself into," he stiffly explained. "You can't understand. There is no escaping—this is what a princess must learn to steel herself against. You will eventually learn to ignore most people. Until then . . . it will be hard."

She looked up at him in horror.

"You mean I'm stuck here in my apartment until I can bring myself to face that mob?"

The veteran reporters had positioned themselves across the street from the unassuming apartment building, lounging on the curb and on the tops of their cars. The cameramen nursed disposable cups of coffee and shooed away curious children who crept too close to their equipment. Some of the royalty watchers, despairing of ever getting a chance of seeing the bride-to-be, much less their real idol, the prince, were sitting on the lawn.

"The prince's limousine!"

The word galvanized the crowd. Reporters abandoned their gossip, and a dozen coffees were spilled out onto the sidewalk. To their feet, cameras whirring and young girls shouting giddily, the mob parted so that the limousine could glide to a graceful stop at the curb in front of the building where *she* lived.

Somehow respectful enough of the trappings of royalty, no one pounded on the smoky glass windows or attempted to scale the hood of the limousine. Nonetheless, their deference wasn't so great that reporters stopped themselves from shouting questions or teens from hurling bouquets of flowers and autograph notebooks—even though, because of the darkened glass, no one was certain that the prince was even in the back seat.

"She's coming out!"

"There she is!"

Attention to the limousine was abandoned—the throng galloped to the sidewalk, tumbling over themselves as they created a pencil-thin path for her to walk through.

"We love you, Aleta!" a gaggle of teenaged girls shouted.

"Face shielded by the brim of a...looks like a Chanel hat," a woman reporter said quietly into her dictaphone. "Aleta Clayton walked quickly as she approached the sleek black stretch limousine which will take her to her next tryst with the prince. The Chicago secretary has captured the hearts of..."

The princess-to-be held the brim of her hat down low upon her face as she briskly negotiated her way to the car.

"Give us a smile!" photographers shrieked.

"Will you be attending the mayor's celebration at Navy Pier this evening?" a reporter cried.

"Over here, Princess! Into the camera—a nice, bright smile, please."

"We love you, Aleta!"

"When did you realize you were in love with the prince?"

But the princess-to-be refused to acknowledge the mob with anything other than a brief, surreptitious wave as one of the prince's aides opened the limousine door and she slipped inside. Her smile, already seen in magazines around the world, was covered entirely by her hat.

The reporters and cameramen hastened to their minivans and rented cars—peeling rubber as they followed the limousine away from the quiet residential neighborhood. The fans dissipated, having gotten their glimpse of rare royalty.

No one noticed a second limousine pulling out of the alley behind the apartment building.

As they pulled away from the alley, free from the pursuers, Aleta relaxed into the buttery leather seat of the limousine and began to laugh.

"What's so funny?" the prince asked.

"Maggie. I bet she's having a wonderful time—it'll be the first time she's ever been driven by a chauffeur," Aleta said. "When she started dating, her mother was so protective that she drove Maggie to all her dates. So Maggie took to sitting in the back seat and pretending that her mother was merely a chauffeur. But that's not quite the same thing as really being in a limousine."

Hortensio looked back from his perch in the front seat to smile at her story.

"So, where are we going?" Aleta asked. "Do you want to play miniature golf? I know a place that . . ."

The prince shook his head.

"The airport," he said.

Aleta's eyes widened with surprise and delight.

He was taking her away! In an instant, her head was filled with images of a getaway weekend—someplace isolated where they could be by themselves.

"The airport! Why didn't you tell me? I would have packed a bag," she added excitedly. "Where are you taking me?"

Giancarlo looked away.

"Nowhere," he said. "I have to fly to Washington for a meeting with the ambassador."

Aleta felt a hardening lump develop in her throat.

Without meaning to, she had a sudden stab of jealousy—not for the ambassador, of course, but for the possibility—should she say probability?—that there would be another woman in Washington.

One who wasn't so suitable, but a lot more fun.

"Why didn't you tell me?"

The prince shrugged.

"I could have gone with you," Aleta added, although it hurt her pride to admit that he had purposely excluded her.

"If you're having trouble adjusting to the pace of public appearances, now's not the time for me to take you to Washington," he said, patting her arm reassuringly. "Besides, you have a million and one things to do with my mother to plan the wedding."

Aleta nodded morosely.

"I'll be in Monticello by Wednesday," he added. "Our wedding will be held on Friday. You will travel back with my mother tomorrow afternoon to Monticello. Passport restrictions have been waived already. You will, I trust, be available to accompany the queen to the benefit being hosted at the Ritz Carlton Hotel this evening?"

Aleta slumped back into her seat.

"Why didn't you tell me about your trip?" she asked, not quite able to believe the level of planning—for her life and for his—that had occurred without her knowledge.

"She needs a secretary," Hortensio interrupted. "It is hardly to be expected that she would be able to keep track of her..."

"Oh! Stay out of this, Hortensio," Aleta said angrily, jamming her finger against the button that operated a glass curtain between the front and back seats. The divider slid into place. Within seconds, that imminently practical aide was consigned to passing out his gems of advice to the driver.

The betrothed couple sat in gloomy silence while they passed through the expressway traffic.

"Giancarlo, do I really have to have a secretary to find out what my fiancé is doing?" she asked quietly. "Or even to find out what I'm doing?"

He looked at her, studying her face as if for the first time. As he did, Aleta shivered. He had become so hard, so distant, so much like the arrogant royal that the press hated.

"You don't seem to understand the reason for this marriage," he said at last. "There is a lot more at stake than there usually is."

"I thought the reason why we were getting married was the reason everyone else gets married," she said, hating the petulant tone of her voice. "I thought it was love."

"First of all, we are not like 'everyone else,'" Giancarlo explained. "But, even so, people marry for all sorts of reasons—security, friendship, children."

"Why are you getting married?" she asked, noticing quite clearly that he had avoided the one word that she had been waiting to hear from his lips ever since she had said yes.

Love.

"You want me to say that I love you," Giancarlo accused quietly. And, within her, Aleta knew that he was right. "But that love isn't what makes me marry—it is my duty to my country which makes me marry."

She felt as deflated as a pricked balloon. Of course, it had been outrageous for her to believe that, in scant days, she had captured the heart of the most celebrated bachelor of the late twentieth century when women more glamorous, more beautiful, more charming had failed. And it was equally arrogant of her to believe that their whirlwind rush to the altar was the result of love and not a dynastic obligation.

"Why are you marrying me?" Giancarlo asked quietly, interrupting her gloomy thoughts.

Tears sprang to her eyes.

"Because I love you," she said and then hesitated. The differences between the man she loved from afar, the man she had spent a magical day with, and the man who sat next to her in the car had never seemed more stark. "But you think that's not true?"

"What about me do you love?" he asked, tenderly brushing away her tears. "The things you've read about me? My exploits on the polo fields, on the ski slopes? Or is it my title, my wealth, my position on the *International Snoop*'s most eligible bachelor list?"

"No, no, no!" Aleta shook her head forcefully. "It was never those things—oh, all right, maybe it was at first. But I love the man I walked with on the beach. I love the man I talked to that afternoon. I love the man I ate hot dogs with. I love the man I shared a blanket with," she added, blushing miserably at the memory that must mean nothing to him and everything to her.

"Well, that's me, all right," Giancarlo said.

"So then, what's the problem?" Aleta cried out.

"Unfortunately, that's not the man you're going to marry."

"What do you mean?"

"The man you are to marry is driven by responsibilities and ambitions for his country." His voice rose with anger. "The man you will marry works grueling fifteen- and sixteen-hour days and doesn't get what the average man thinks of as a vacation. The man you will marry is tied up with the obligations of being a head of state—a small state, but one that is nonetheless important to its citizens." He paused briefly. "And you wouldn't be marrying me if I wasn't that man."

"I would, too!" Aleta cried out.

"Would you have read articles about me in magazines and newspapers if I were a waiter in a deli? Would you have let Hortensio talk you into a dinner at the Pump Room with an anonymous auto mechanic? Would you have a poster of me hanging in your bedroom if I were a fireman?"

His accusation made her blush—he had noticed the giant Prince Giancarlo poster hanging on the door of her closet.

But she also blushed because he had hit upon a larger truth, one that she had hidden from her consciousness.

She wouldn't have fallen for him so hard, so early, so long if he were a waiter, an auto mechanic, a fireman.

Her mother had raised her to be a princess and her mother must have known that Aleta wouldn't settle for anyone less than a prince for her husband.

How can I complain about him acting or thinking or talking like a prince when I'm just as guilty? Aleta wondered. The irony that Giancarlo—the entire world, for that matter—thought he was marrying an average commoner would have struck her as funny. If she weren't about to cry.

"You said you were marrying me because of obligation," she began. "So, I'm just a figurehead, aren't I? A wife at the castle while you…" She couldn't finish her thought.

"Just because you're my wife doesn't mean I can't love you," he said. "I love the woman I walked with, I talked with, I ate a hot dog with."

She startled at his words, the words she had hungered for for so long.

"You do? You love me?"

He nodded.

"But I know that the woman I love is very different from who the woman I marry will be."

"How…?"

"The woman I marry is poised and elegant, gracious and charming…."

"I am?"

"You are now, and you'll be more so as you grow into your position," he said. "And the woman I love existed for me on that one day—but the way our lives are set up, that woman won't be with me again."

"You make it sound so grim."

"I have lived with the obligations of my…position for so long that I've given up being depressed about its constraints."

He slipped his hand into hers, squeezing her fingers in a tender gesture that was meant to reassure, but only succeeded in depressing her even further. Within minutes, they were at the airport, driving through a private road directly to the Monticello jet that would whisk him away.

"I will see you in Monticello the day before our wedding," Giancarlo said, and kissed her cheek. The gentle touch of his lips was like a funeral for her hopes. "I wish..."

The glass that separated the two sections of the car slid down and Hortensio turned to speak with them.

"Your Highness, we must hurry. We have been given permission for immediate take-off and we must take advantage of that."

Giancarlo nodded, his face returning to the cool, masculine mask of strength, of one upon whom others depend.

"Of course, Hortensio," he said.

Aleta knew that she shouldn't prolong their goodbye. He did have responsibilities, worries that extended far beyond the small, simple matters of courtship.

"Goodbye, Giancarlo."

He started to organize his papers and then stopped.

"You know, I have always wanted to know how my subjects live," he said. "Every year I go to harvest festivals, jewel shops, banks and all kinds of other tours. But I wonder sometimes what those people do when they aren't dressed for their prince, smiling for their prince or when they're not gawking at me. I wonder how the harvest works, how the jewels are cut, what the tellers do during their lunch hours."

She stared at him, wondering at the words he spoke.

"But now I have learned something so interesting," he continued. "I don't know how my own subjects spend their days—but I know how an average American spends a day with his girl."

His words cut through her with a knife of sadness.

How much he had missed in all his years of privilege!

But there was no time for mourning his wealth and position. From behind him, she could see the pilot at the cockpit door, motioning for the party to hurry. Hortensio grabbed at the prince's sleeve.

"Goodbye, Giancarlo."

"Goodbye, Aleta."

So final.

So absolute.

The wedding of the decade was turning into the nightmare of her life. She was marrying a man who believed that their marriage was nothing more than a treaty, a dynastic covenant. She watched him stride across the tarmac, so virile and strong—no wonder women adored him. And yet, could they see within him, did they care to see within him? Had any woman ever seen him as she had? Had any woman known that there was a part of him so desperate for a moment of a commoner's life?

He turned briefly to wave before he disappeared within the plane. Hortensio nodded in the direction of the limousine.

"Where to, madame?" the driver asked, as the plane began to rev its engines.

"Anywhere," she said. "Just drive . . . anywhere."

Chapter Nine

"Do you think Maurice D'Algernon himself is actually going to do the final fittings in Monticello?" Maggie asked, excitedly pirouetting in front of the gilded mirror. The pale yellow chiffon skirt, beaded with gold and pearls, swirled about her legs. "I read in *Snoop* that each of these dresses costs over $15,000. That's probably more than the bridesmaids' gowns for Liz Taylor's last wedding."

"Thank God we don't have to pay for our outfits," Rhoda said as she slipped the luxurious fabric over her head. "The last wedding I was a bridesmaid for, I spent almost five hundred dollars by the time I had my dress, my shoes, my wrap. George was ready to kill me."

"Ooooooohh!" Carla squealed as she slipped into her dress. "I can barely believe that we're all going to be bridesmaids at a royal wedding. As I was saying on *Good Morning Chicago...*"

The inert figure on the pink chaise lounge roused herself.

"Good Morning Chicago?"

"Oh, Aleta, it was nothing," Carla explained, her face suddenly blanketed with worry. "I didn't say anything new—they just asked me three questions. What were you like as a co-worker, what is the prince like and what do I know about plans for the wedding?"

"Oh, who cares?" Aleta muttered and lay back down.

"And then they asked me to tell them a little about how we all knew that you guys are in love," Carla continued. "I just told them it was obvious."

Aleta stared up at her.

"From how you guys look," Carla finished lamely. "I mean, you guys are in love, aren't you? This isn't one of those arranged marriages, is it?"

"Carla!" Maggie shrieked. "Why don't you take your foot out of your mouth and try on your shoes?"

Imperious as any royal, Maggie led Carla into the dressing room of the Ambassador East suite that had become Aleta's "home" since the prince had left and her apartment had been surrounded.

Boxes, marked with swank European return addresses, had begun arriving at noon—bridesmaids' dresses, stockings, gloves, veils, hats, shoes, extra outfits for the myriad social events planned for the week of the wedding. Aleta recalled that a few days earlier, the queen had asked her what color she would want for her wedding and Aleta had thought of sunny, happy yellow. A perfect foil for her true feelings.

Her vague wish had become the command of some of Paris and Milan's finest designers.

The wedding dress itself hung limply on the back of the door to the bathroom, still in its protective plastic sheath. Aleta hadn't yet had the energy to try it on.

"Honey, how come you look so depressed?" Rhoda asked, plopping down on an armchair with a great *swoooosh!* of the airy fabric of her bridesmaid's dress. "For a bride, you don't look so hot. You're supposed to be happy, radiant, dancing on air. Or at least, so anxious that you can't sit still."

Aleta stared at the ceiling of the sitting room. She had virtually memorized the overhead mural of clouds and angels and banners announcing all sorts of things in Latin, but it was better to study the artwork than look straight in the eye at Rhoda.

"You're going to lose him," Rhoda announced, arranging her skirt about her lap.

"What do you mean?" Aleta said dully. "We're getting married—I'd hardly call that losing him."

"Anger," Rhoda said. "That's a good start."

Aleta shook her head.

"I'm not angry. And what do you mean?"

Rhoda leaned forward and took Aleta's hand into her own. The sudden and unexpected human contact made Aleta feel like crying. The past few days had been spent at parties, receptions, luncheons and openings. Through it all, there hadn't been a single instant when anyone had seen beyond the expected happiness of a soon-to-be princess into the heart of a very sad and very lonely young woman. Her plastered-on smile fooled even the most jaded royalty watcher.

Fooled everyone except Rhoda.

"You aren't fighting for your man," her friend said.

"There isn't any other woman. At least, not that I know of," she added. Giancarlo had, she admitted, phoned each evening during his Washington trip, though the conversations had been somewhat strained. Her anger at what she assumed were his "duty" calls to her made her unresponsive at best and sometimes quietly hostile at her worst.

It was a wonder he had called back.

But, of course he would, she thought bitterly. It was his duty and Giancarlo always performed his duties well.

There had never been any evidence of "extracurricular interests" in these calls. There had been no time of the day or night that she had not known his whereabouts—she had been so familiar with his schedule that she was starting to think that she knew Washington well, even though she had never been there.

Besides, she admitted, the press was keeping such close tabs on him that an illicit tryst would have been impossible for him or his aides to arrange.

"It's not about other women and it's not about getting the ring—being married doesn't mean that you don't have to fight anymore for your man and not having a woman vying for his attention doesn't mean you've got him."

Aleta was confused.

"Let me explain," Rhoda said, pulling Aleta up into a seated position. "You aren't very happy, you'll admit?"

Aleta shook her head. There was no point in denying Rhoda's words.

"And you're doubting yourself, doubting this marriage?"

Aleta nodded.

"I feel terrible," she admitted. "All these people want me to be married, want the best for me, and I'm simply scared. Sometimes I think I'm making a terrible mistake. But I have no idea how to get out of it—and I'm not even sure that I'd want to. You don't understand. I've known I would marry him since I was nine years old.''

She wiped away a tear that had fallen to her cheek.

Rhoda reached to the occasional table and took one of the linen-and-lace handkerchiefs that had been shipped to the suite. The expensive squares of cloth were a far cry from the paper tissues that either of them had used—before royalty came to call.

"Might as well use it," Rhoda said, as she gave Aleta the handkerchief.

A squeal of delight from the other room startled both of them, but after waiting a few seconds, they realized they would not be interrupted. Carla and Maggie were too busy admiring themselves to worry about confidences shared in the other room.

"You have to fight for your man," Rhoda said. "And I'm scared you've given up too early. You have a great foundation, better than most people have. And yet you're squandering it because you're unwilling to fight for your love."

"That sounds like advice you give a woman who couldn't get a guy to propose."

"Honey, a married woman has to fight for her husband's love every day, every bit as much as a single girl. In my own marriage, I've had to fight for George's love. And sometimes, I've wondered if it's all worth it. I always end up deciding that it is."

"I didn't know you and George fought."

"Silly girl!" she teased, and tousled Aleta's hair. Without meaning to, Aleta felt a surge of optimism course through her. "I don't have to fight against

George—I have to fight against boredom, against the demands of the kids and work, against the kind of drifting apart that so many long-term marriages suffer from. I have to assess the battlefield and the enemy—and every day it's a new one.''

"Yeah, but why is it your job to do the fighting?" Aleta asked. "Why isn't it George's job, too?"

"Men don't know how to fight for their woman." Rhoda laughed. "They think you punch out the guy who's flirting with her or show her that you know how to fix a flat tire—the average guy thinks that's how you fight for a relationship. And I'd bet even princes think that way, too."

"Rhoda, you're pretty sexist."

"Honey, you can be sexist and realistic about the limits of your man," Rhoda warned. "Or you can expect someone else to save your relationship for you—and watch it float right out the window."

If it hasn't already gone, Aleta thought grimly.

"I don't know enough about you and the prince to tell you what your enemy is," Rhoda continued. "Only you can do that."

The enemy? Aleta wondered. She couldn't, just wouldn't, admit to Rhoda that the worry that plagued her, that wouldn't let her sleep at night, that wouldn't let her feel the joy that every bride feels.

Wife material. I'm wife material.

How could she possibly fight against that?

Carla and Maggie wafted into the room, their chiffon skirts trailing behind them.

"You're so lucky, Aleta!" Carla exclaimed. "To be marrying a handsome prince. Are you going to do all the things we talked about—like have all your clothes made by Chanel and spend every day at the beach and sleep until noon?''

Aleta didn't have the heart to tell Carla that those were the things that Rhoda, Maggie and Carla herself had thought they would do if they were princesses. *I'll spend my days cutting ribbons and giving speeches on the importance of agriculture,* Aleta thought to herself, *and my nights will be spent...*

She looked at Rhoda and then at Carla.

How am I going to back out of this now, Aleta thought grimly, *now that the dress from Paris has already been sent? Now that the heads of states around the world have RSVPed? Now that the Monticello cathedral is being readied? Now that three million Monticellans are thinking they can breathe a sigh of relief about the future of their nation—free from Spain's interference?*

"Come on, you gotta try that dress on," Carla said. "It's the most beautiful..." She patted her eyes with a handkerchief. "You know, Aleta, it's the biggest, most beautiful, wedding of the year, of the decade, of the..."

"No, I don't feel like it quite yet," she said, shaking her head. "But why don't you try on the dresses they sent over for the fireworks display for the evening before the wedding?"

The offer was so tantalizing that Maggie and Carla completely forgot any fleeting suspicions they might have had regarding their soon-to-be-married friend. If they thought she seemed unhappy, if they thought she was unnaturally reluctant to try on her dress—those thoughts disappeared as soon as they reached into the wardrobe trunks for the silk-and-lace ballgowns that Maurice D'Algernon's designer shop had sent over.

* * *

She had never liked to fly, had always been frightened of taking off. Or was it that she was more frightened by landing? The few times that she had flown, Aleta had clutched the arms of her seat and prayed for a safe journey.

But she was not frightened as the queen's private jet took off from O'Hare International Airport. A tenacious crowd had followed the queen and the princess-to-be from the Ambassador East to the airport and even onto the tarmac. Well-wishers, curiosity seekers, reporters, photographers, politicians hoping for a last handshake memorialized for the voters.

Until airport security arrived to push the crowd back, Aleta had thought she would be trampled. As it was, the sleeve of her jacket had been torn and her feet stepped on so many times she was certain they would swell a full size.

The jet was a welcome relief—quiet and calm even as it sped down the runway. Aleta was relieved to leave the mobs behind.

The queen had unbuckled herself as soon as they reached cruising altitude and had excused herself to her private bedroom onboard. Aleta's newly hired secretary, Ananda, led Aleta to her own surprisingly spacious room.

"Is there anything I can get you, Your Highness?" Ananda asked.

Aleta simply stared at the bed and its luxurious peach-colored silk comforter. A nap—a quiet sleep—would be wonderful! After all, it would be a full twelve hours before they reached Monticello.

"Maybe a cup of tea," Aleta stated.

Ananda disappeared and Aleta kicked off her shoes. She settled into the bed, and when Ananda arrived moments later with a cup of tea, Aleta was already asleep.

Hours later, Aleta awoke. Ananda sat at a nearby chair, reading a book. Aleta stared at her for a few moments, thinking to herself that the pretty, dark-haired girl was just like herself—well, a Monticello version of herself.

A typical Monticello girl, Aleta thought. I used to be a typical American girl.

"Did you sleep well?"

Aleta started to shake her head no, but then reconsidered. The disturbing dreams about Giancarlo were really no different from the ones that had plagued her every night. Dreams of longing met with his rejection of her.

Was she making a horrible mistake to marry?

It certainly seemed that way.

And yet, there seemed no way to get off the track, off the speeding trail to her wedding.

"I slept very well, thank you."

"Wonderful. The queen is still sleeping but the chef has already prepared dinner. Her Majesty encourages you to eat when you feel ready."

Aleta's stomach growled in response, although the noise of the jet's engines prevented her secretary from hearing.

"I'd love some dinner, but would you join me?"

There was a moment's flicker of hesitation—what a violation of protocol this would be!—and then the girl agreed.

Within minutes, an elegant meal of beef tournedos and vegetables sautéed in wine was delivered to the cabin by a uniformed steward. Not the usual airliner food, Aleta thought wryly as she unfolded her napkin and studied the ornate Monticellan seal on the china.

Over their meal, the two women quickly developed an unexpected camaraderie. Women's lives so often share the same elements—regardless of the country—and the two were quickly swapping stories of family, friends, schools, work and men.

Aleta, mindful of the delicacy of her situation, listened when Ananda spoke of her boyfriend, who was a student at the Monticello Universidad, and her former suitors. But the two women seemed to understand that speaking of the prince must be off-limits.

"What do you and your boyfriend do on a typical Friday night?" Aleta asked.

"Oh, we usually go to the Palacio Teatro for a movie and then maybe stop at one of the clubs. Not any of the ones in Monticello City," she added. "Those are always overrun with tourists and they're too expensive for my salary or my boyfriend's scholarship money. We go outside the city—to the places in the mountains. Less crowded, less expensive, less . . ."

Ananda continued to speak, but Aleta didn't hear. Her thoughts were far away from the jet speeding to her new home. She was back at the Ambassador East, in the arms of her friend Rhoda. Fighting for her man, fighting for anything, seemed so foreign to her. After all, for years Mr. McCormick had berated her for a hundred things that he was wrong about. And she had never stood up to him. Somehow the fight had gone out of her when her mother had died.

But wouldn't her mother want her to fight—now more than ever?

Monticello security forces arranged for a quiet reunion for the couple at the airport. The media was informed by the palace that the prince and his bride-to-be would be available for photos the next morning. And, because Monticello was a country where newspapers had coexisted with royalty for centuries under a loosely negotiated treaty that simultaneously guaranteed privacy and great photo opportunities, the press had deferred.

Therefore, the terminal where Hortensio and Giancarlo waited was virtually empty—the hourly planeloads of tourists and the personal jets of visiting billionaires being routed to another section of the airport.

"What time is it?" Giancarlo asked as he paced the marble floor.

"Two and a half minutes later than the last time you asked," Hortensio said calmly. Hortensio was reading the local paper and he didn't look up when his patron spoke.

"I don't think you're acting appropriately deferential to a prince," Giancarlo said with mock severity.

"All right." Hortensio shrugged, looking up from his paper briefly, "Your Highness, it is two and a half minutes later than the last time you asked."

The two men shared a laugh and Giancarlo stopped his pacing long enough to stare out at the sun-drenched runway.

"How long before she gets here?" he asked, consciously trying to keep his frustration and impatience hidden.

"I shall call the tower again," Hortensio said, and folded his newspaper.

While Hortensio went to the courtesy phone, Giancarlo continued to stare at the empty runway. His anxiety about their coming reunion was increasing rapidly. He hadn't even been this nervous for his crowning.

What would he discover when she walked from the airplane into his arms?

Or, at least, he hoped she would walk into his arms.

Would he discover that she was cheerful, happy to be home in her adopted country, happy to be with the man she would call her husband? Not likely, he admitted, since the phone calls that they had shared had become increasingly stilted—filled with minutiae about this or that function or ceremony. Would she pout as she appeared on the tarmac? No, no, Aleta never pouted. Would she be distant, somehow keeping a part of herself held back from him even as she passively allowed him to take her into his arms?

That was more like Aleta, he thought.

He was resigned, by duty, to marry a woman he might have loved under different circumstances. Although, come to think of it, in ordinary circumstances he was swept up by the flashy charms of the glittering jet set so it was unlikely that he would have sat still long enough to get to know Aleta.

In ordinary circumstances.

Nonetheless, this marriage was merely another duty, such as setting tariffs on imported products and attending ceremonial functions. His mother had devoted every moment to her country, and there really wasn't any reason he shouldn't.

So where was the problem? Why was he so morose, why was he so grim? Why did this particular duty cause him so much pain?

Perhaps because I would have liked a marriage unfettered by these concerns, he thought, realizing for the first time that had there been no royal reason for marriage, he might actually have already wed.

Meanwhile, half the world celebrated his intended nuptials and already he dreaded them—dreaded them all the more because he thought he might love her. Might love her and he knew that little love would be quickly crushed by the duties attendant with this marriage.

Or rather, his inability to discharge this particular duty without resentment.

There were other marriages, marriages of royalty, that had turned out poorly with much more auspicious beginnings and Giancarlo wondered if he was being consigned to the fate of many of his titled and wealthy friends.

A chilly marriage scrutinized in embarrassing detail by the press.

But dammit, he loved her. Or, at least, he had loved her until he had realized that the marriage they would have wouldn't be part of what they had carved out for themselves on a wondrous Chicago day. He had loved her for the briefest of moments when he had forgotten that she was, however innocently, part of the sticky web of duty that threatened to choke off anything spontaneous, anything personal, anything wonderful in his life.

She was, in short, wonderful wife material.

That was the point.

Wife material and certainly not a woman he would spend fun times with.

He had looked with revulsion at the shipping magnates, the counts and kings, the sheiks and sultans who spent their money and their time with a never-ending stream of young, beautiful, frivolous women while their own wives suffered at home. Suffered through expensive shopping trips and perhaps their own dalliances—but suffered nonetheless from the humiliations their husbands brought them. He had always found those men disgusting—and yet, he looked at his future and knew he had a great likelihood of turning into just that sort of man.

"It's too bad we're not in a bar and there's a guy flirting with her," he said aloud.

"Huh?" Hortensio asked, appearing noiselessly at his side. "What did you say?"

"I said that I thought it was too bad that we're not in a bar and there's a guy flirting with Aleta."

Hortensio's face scrunched up with puzzlement.

"Then I'd punch the guy, wipe my bloodied hands on my mechanic's overalls and that would be that," Giancarlo added.

Hortensio nodded. He understood.

"Or I wish that I could show her that I can do something important," Giancarlo mused.

"I think negotiating the development deal with..."

"No, no, Hortensio. Something more tangible than that. Fixing a flat tire, or something."

Hortensio shrugged.

"I'd fix a flat tire," Giancarlo mused. "I'd push a car out of a snowbank with my bare hands. And that would be that. Nothing complicated in a relationship that I wouldn't be able to solve with some muscle and some brawn. Wouldn't it be wonderful if the world worked that way?"

"I don't know how to advise you on this, Your Highness," he said. "But I do know that the royal jet is taxiing down the runway."

Giancarlo looked out onto the tarmac and saw the jet glide to a halt. He had been so busy thinking of his own concerns that he hadn't noticed the Monticello royal jet landing.

"Time to go see her," Hortensio said.

"I guess you're right," Giancarlo answered, now dreading the meeting with his fiancée.

He walked across the tarmac, followed closely by Hortensio. As the doors to the jet opened and the stairwell was positioned, he saw her—and he thought for a moment that his troubles were over, that she was his and that he was ready to be hers.

It wasn't just that Aleta was beautiful. She was, there was no question that she was. And the past few weeks of being taken in hand by the world's most demanding experts in cosmetics, clothing and hairstyling had changed the chrysalis into a truly magnificent butterfly.

It wasn't that Aleta was royal material. Although, certainly, in the time that he had known her, she had learned to walk with her head erect, her shoulders squared and with a poise that would do any kingdom proud.

But she looked at him from the door of the jet's cabin with a tentativeness that communicated that she, too, had been feeling the same doubts that he had—and that she wanted, as he did, to put those doubts to rest. She wanted to be his wife and she wanted to make being his wife a joy.

As he neared the stairwell, his heart lifted with delight. Perhaps there was no stranger flirting with his woman whom he could punch, perhaps there was no car to fix. But maybe he didn't need those things.

She was looking at him with a wary welcome, a welcome to her own country, a nation with only two possible citizens. And, for the briefest of moments, he thought they had succeeded in smoothing the course before them.

"Your Highness, can we get a shot of you smooching with your honey?"

Giancarlo turned in horror at the loudly dressed man who shoved a camera toward him. Three more reporters with their own cameras crouched behind their leader, ready to record the damage done by the bad-boy prince if he punched the man first.

"Damn, it's the *International Snoop*'s Monticello bureau, all four of them," Hortensio cried. "They think the First Amendment to the American constitution follows them out of their own country and onto our soil!"

"Hey, all we want is a picture of them kissing. We gotta right to that."

As the reporters scuffled with Hortensio at the stairwell, Giancarlo looked up at Aleta. She was being hustled by other security personnel toward the back exit of the jet. The last moment that their eyes made contact, her eyes were clouded over. She had thought they would start anew in Monticello. *She must think she's wrong,* Giancarlo thought. *She must think our whole lives together will be like this.* She must think that reporters would follow and harass them as diligently as they had other royal marriages that had slid into trouble so quickly.

"Dammit, I've had enough!" he shouted and turned around to punch the reporter directly behind him on the stairwell. A flurry of camera whirring confirmed for him that this week's *Snoop* would have appalling pictures of him—but he didn't care. He regarded only briefly the injured reporter who now lay on the tarmac.

Then he wiped his hands on his pants and ran to catch up with the limousine that had rushed to the back exit of the jet.

Chapter Ten

"You can either wear the red dress or the blue dress to the dinner and fireworks this evening," Ananda announced, holding up the two dresses for Aleta to choose. "If you wear the red that means you'll have to wear the blue on your first evening in Australia, which might be a good idea. On the other hand, if you wear the blue..."

Aleta shrugged an I-don't-care, and Ananda decided that the red gown was best after all. Aleta had been through the same discussion so many times in Chicago that this choice didn't hold any excitement for her.

Her mind was on other plans besides the dinner and the late-night fireworks display that would be viewed from the palace balcony.

She stepped into the gown and allowed her secretary to button the red dress and hand her the matching accessories. A hairdresser had already twisted her hair into an elegant French twist. Her jewels, a small diamond necklace and matching earrings which were made for a minor Hapsburg princess of the last century, had been sent to her palace apartment by the queen.

Twenty minutes later, she was in the dining room, listening with half an ear to the chatter of the American ambassador at her left. A hundred and fifty guests crowded at the table that stretched as far in either direction as Aleta could see. Kings, queens, prime ministers and presidents were in attendance.

Her bridesmaids, all bookkeepers from McCormick Industrial Supply Company, were at the other end of the table.

But Aleta was only interested in one other diner.

To her right, the prince seemed distracted—the guest to his right had nearly given up engaging him in conversation. He stared into his plate and nodded disinterestedly at his dinner partner. Aleta thought she might be the princess of Denmark.

Aleta had learned a lot about etiquette in the past few weeks. She knew to bow to the queen first thing upon entering the room. She knew to wait until her dinner partner had pulled her seat out from under the table before she sat down. She knew which fork to use for the salmon *en croute* that she was trying to interest herself in.

She also knew that she was supposed to speak to whomever was seated at her left until the next course was served. Then, over that course, she was to turn her attention to the prince. When the waiters took those plates away, the American ambassador at her left must rightfully claim her attention once more.

Back and forth, back and forth.

Although she didn't pay attention to what the American ambassador was telling her, she tried to nod and smile at appropriate intervals—all the while hoping that the soup would come soon.

It was soup that was coming next, wasn't it? After so many courses, Aleta was starting to lose track.

At last, her plate was taken and replaced with a bowl of ginger-beef bouillon.

"Enjoying yourself?" the prince asked.

Aleta nodded as she sipped at the fragrant soup.

"The fireworks will be tiring," Giancarlo admitted. "But since Monticello is one of Europe's leading producers of fireworks, we really must . . ."

"Meet me after dessert at the back of the lower kitchen door," Aleta interrupted quickly, keeping her tone as pleasant as if she was pointing out something amusing to the prince.

"What?"

"Keep your voice down, darling," she said sweetly. "Everyone wants to hear what you have to say. You don't want others to overhear our tender words of love, do you?"

He looked about and discovered she was right. People had abruptly stopped their conversation to look at the couple. But, being caught eavesdropping by the prince himself, they returned to their food, their dinner partners, their own concerns.

Aleta took a deep breath. What she was doing was taking more courage than she had ever thought she had.

"I told you to meet me after dessert at the back of the lower kitchen door," she repeated in a near whisper. "I want to spend some time with you alone before the wedding."

"The fireworks will end at 2:00 a.m.—we could meet then," he offered. "At least for a few minutes."

Aleta shook her head.

"After dessert."

"That's absolutely ridiculous," Giancarlo hissed. "I can't leave. My mother is expecting us, the press is expecting us, we have half the dignitaries of..."

"I don't care," Aleta said, desperately modulating her voice and her smile to give the impression to onlookers of carefree delight. "I asked you to meet me at the back of the kitchen door."

"Nobody tells a prince what to do."

Aleta stared up at him, unable to keep the anger from her eyes.

Of all the priggish, boorish...

But a glance at a few curious onlookers across the table and she turned her face quickly into a mask of adoration.

"My dear prince, *everyone* tells you what to do," she said quietly, and leaned over to put her head near his shoulder as if sharing a tender confidence. "That's the whole point. You have so many responsibilities you can only listen to them—as communicated by Hortensio or the queen or the banks or the parliament. You always do exactly what responsibility tells you to do. I'm simply asking you to listen for once to someone else."

His face flushed, but she didn't have time to find out if it was anger or shame that fueled him. A waiter had taken her soup and another was approaching with roast duck with black cherry and orange sauce.

"Meet me," she said sotto voce, and turned with a brilliant smile to the American ambassador. "So, how long have you been in Monticello?"

She felt Giancarlo bristling at her right side throughout the main course. With a little concentration, she noticed that he barely managed a polite series of comments to the chatter of the woman to his right. And every time his leg brushed against hers she thought she felt the electric spark of anger coursing through him.

But she was fighting for her happiness, for her marriage, for her life. *And there is no way,* she thought as she stared across the table at a morose and lonely princess who had once seemed the subject of a latter-day fairy tale, *there is no way that I will end up like her.*

The newest course presented, a light and airy soufflé, the engaged couple was again allowed to speak to one another.

"I cannot walk away from my responsibilities this evening," the prince said quietly. "What would the queen think?"

"I think the queen will be busy entertaining her guests."

"And what about those guests?"

"I think the guests can understand an engaged couple *in love*—" she emphasized the two words "—wanting to spend time with each other. Besides, they'll be concentrating on the fireworks."

"What about the press?"

"It's dark. I hardly think that your absence at the balcony will be noticed, and besides . . ." She paused to let her words sink in. "Besides, you won't be getting married tomorrow morning if you don't meet me."

He stared at her in horror, and then, as conversation about them halted, he recovered with a smile and a light kiss to Aleta's forehead. His gesture was met by a round of murmured *oohs* and *aahs.*

"You can't be serious," he whispered as his lips met her forehead.

"I'm utterly serious," she said as she looked up at him with ostentatious adoration.

"I won't be blackmailed."

"I won't be pushed."

She wanted to add that she wouldn't be pushed into a loveless marriage. She would fight, but, if she had to, she would have no choice but to retreat.

Permanently.

But did she really have the courage to stun the world with a broken engagement? Especially when the damnably sexy man beside her was, in fact, the only man she had ever loved?

The queen had stood. The guests, Aleta and the prince included, placed their napkins at their places and rose as one to watch her depart from the room, through the glass doors that led directly to the balcony.

"May I escort you to your place at the balcony?" The American ambassador offered. "The fireworks are to begin in minutes."

Aleta shook her head.

"Please go ahead," she suggested. "I shall be detained for a moment."

The ambassador joined the crowd that surged toward the doors leading to the balcony.

Aleta looked about, but didn't see the prince.

Perhaps he wouldn't meet her. Perhaps he didn't believe that she would leave the palace, leave him, if he didn't.

And she herself wasn't even sure that she could bring herself to leave, to make good on the threat.

Every possible choice was frightening.

If he would just meet her. . . .

She raced up to her apartment and hastily changed into the casual black pants and sweater that she had made Ananda lay out for her. Slipping out of her high heels, she was grateful for the flats that Ananda had thoughtfully provided.

Then Aleta slipped down the back stairs, through the kitchen, past the startled help, and into the alley that ran between the palace and the servants' quarters.

Please make him show up, she prayed silently, as she got into the driver's seat of Ananda's car and waited for him.

But the minutes were long. And lonely.

Sitting in the darkness, she could hear the fireworks exploding from the distance. She heard the kitchen staff close the pantry, having been given the rest of the evening off to watch the beautiful show.

He wasn't going to come, she realized, letting her head droop to the steering wheel. She felt a tear course down her cheeks. He hadn't taken her seriously. He had been a prince so long that he thought he could order people about and ignore them when they wanted him to do something—he had been a prince so long, that he was...

A not-so-quiet, not-so-ladylike sob erupted from her throat as she realized that she was trapped, that she didn't have the courage to disappoint the world by fleeing, and she didn't have the power to successfully fight for her marriage.

"But I love him!" she cried out.

The passenger door opened and, as her heart leapt from sadness to joy, he slumped into the seat beside her. He wasn't happy, his scowl informed her—he was not at all pleased. There was no reason for him to be. It was, after all, very unusual to be this flagrant in his disregard of royal duty.

But she didn't care. She wanted to jump into the air and shout with delight. Instead, her hands shaking with excitement and nerves, she simply turned the key in the ignition.

"All right, what's this all about?" he asked brusquely. "I understand you have fears about the wedding—you have no idea how much I sympathize. But to endanger the..."

"There's a flashlight and map in the glove compartment," she interrupted.

"Wait a minute, we're not going..."

But the car skidding into the crowded street was her reply. With a grunt of anger, he opened the glove compartment.

Aleta had memorized the first part of the route, and she negotiated easily the traffic that had piled up on the main streets of Monticello City. Thankfully, Ananda had directed her to take the smaller, less congested streets—and, as soon as an opportunity presented itself, Aleta drove into a deserted side street.

"The whole country's watching the fireworks," Giancarlo complained. "I command you to return this car to the palace. Aleta, it looks like you're taking me up into the mountains!"

"Your Highness," Aleta said sweetly. "I'm still an American citizen—at least, until ten o'clock tomorrow morning when we exchange our vows. You can't order me around—when I saw the *Snoop* reporters at the airport, I realized the limits of your power. You can't order me to do anything."

She glanced at him for only a moment. When she did, she was surprised at the horror that had overtaken his face. Aleta suddenly realized that this was a very high-stakes games of chance for her marriage. If she didn't win, if her plan failed... Better not to think of the consequences, she decided.

They drove in silence for several minutes, Aleta only aware of her beating heart, her sweaty fingers gripping at the steering wheel—and the scent of him, the pressure of him, the shadow of him so near to her.

Damn, he made her heart beat faster—he always had. He made her feel so jumpy and excited and it wouldn't change if he loved or if he didn't. *No wonder women fight for him,* she thought.

But I'm going to fight, too.

Not with hysterical tears or manipulative demands. Or threats of suicide, like the deposed Yugoslavian princess was rumored to have done.

She had to fight, even if nothing her mother had ever taught her had prepared her for this.

No one else would fight for their marriage—but Aleta would.

"We're going to the mountains," Aleta confirmed. "Now take off your clothes."

"What!"

She laughed at his disbelief. It was the most wonderfully, deliciously natural laugh she had experienced since she had come to this country.

"I promise I won't watch," she said, with a confident flirtatiousness that was as new as her crown would be. "I have to keep my eyes on the road, remember? Although maybe I'll take a peek," she added slyly.

"But why am I taking my clothes off?" he asked suspiciously.

"Oh, yes, I forgot. There's a change of clothes for you in the back seat. I'd imagine your full-dress formal wear is uncomfortable. I brought along something a little less so."

Without another word, he slid from the front seat to the back. Aleta drove from the city into a winding country path. She could see the blaze of fireworks over the Monticello Bay and hear their booming thunder. A

thousand tiny boats docked at the bay and others
floating beneath the display twinkled and swayed.

Monticello truly was a beautiful country.

"Since I'm resigned to my fate, to my captivity,"
Giancarlo said at her ear, "can I at least ask why you're
doing all this?"

She stopped the car at a ridge overlooking the city.
For a moment, they stared together at the wondrous
celebration of their upcoming wedding.

"I told you I loved you, Giancarlo," she said, conscious of his closeness behind her. Her mother had
never taught her how to battle for the love of her man—
and so her words were unsure—though utterly true. "I
love you and I'm not going to settle for just the prince.
I want the man, as well."

"So, you would take me away from an important
state function? You would interfere with the workings
of our government?"

"Giancarlo, if it were a meeting with your parlia-
mentary council, if you were planning a war with Spain,
I wouldn't spirit you away," she said. "But you think
every minute of your life is available for your country.
And you don't keep anything back for yourself. Even
in marriage, you think you have to give it all to your
country—no wonder you resent me. Can't we take a
part of our lives and make it our own nation? Because
I love you, I'm ready to give this country so much—but
can't we keep something back?"

She turned and looked hesitantly over the seat of the
car. Illuminated by distant explosions, his face was un-
readable. At first she thought he might be angry, or
might have misunderstood what she meant.

But then he leaned forward and, reaching over the
back of her seat, he took her face into his hands.

She knew he had understood.

In the privacy of this night, of this night of a thousand explosions in celebration of their love, he was being asked to throw off his reluctance, his evasiveness, his crown. He was being asked to be a man, to take the love of a woman.

"I don't want to be just your wife," Aleta continued, searching his eyes, illuminated by the fireworks. "I'm not just wife material, I'm not just a woman who happens to have the qualifications of a princess. I want to be yours."

"So I am marrying Aleta and not merely a princess?" he asked.

Her eyes, brimming with tears for the love of a man she had thought she had lost, answered him.

"And if I have to show you how the average man spends his evenings with the average woman again and again, I shall do it," she whispered.

"Even how the average man makes love to the average woman?" Giancarlo challenged.

"You're the one with more experience," she chided hoarsely. "I think you're the one who will be teaching me."

Giancarlo slid over the back of the front seat so that he was beside her. He pulled her into his arms and his lips claimed hers amid a series of fireworks' explosions. Abandoning herself, letting go of weeks of doubt, Aleta opened her mouth and herself to the tantalizing, sparkling moment.

She had fought for her man.

And won.

After creating some of their own fireworks, Giancarlo and Aleta watched more of the official display. Seeing Monticellan nightlife would have to wait—there would be thousands of other nights like these when they'd be able to slip away from the palace.

"This seems to me to be a typical American date," Giancarlo announced. "Dinner, watching a fireworks display and kissing the woman you love."

"I bet it's a typical Monticello date, as well."

An hour later, the prince and his bride-to-be bade farewell to their guests as the fireworks display ended. No one had noticed the royals' absence, but a few noticed that the buttons on the gown of the princess-to-be were not done properly.

These few thought they were wise, and thought they understood things they didn't.

Among them was the queen, who stood later at the window of her bedroom and stared into the gathering morning sky.

"I'm not sure I approve of what happened tonight," she said. "I didn't actually see Giancarlo or Aleta through the whole display and yet, they managed..."

"Don't trouble yourself about it, Your Majesty," a voice declared from the bed. "What matters is that the prince will be married in six hours and you haven't gotten a wink of sleep. Your eyes will have unsightly dark circles if you don't take care of yourself."

"Oh, Hortensio, I guess you're right. You're always right," she said, putting the curtains back together and slipping into bed.

"I'm glad to hear you finally admitting that," Hortensio said, pulling the covers over them both. "Thank you, Your Majesty."

Designer Maurice D'Algernon arrived at the bride-to-be's apartment an hour before the wedding, carrying an emergency sewing kit that he hoped he wouldn't need. His career would be made or broken this day, and he shuddered at the thought that the petite American hadn't been fitted.

"The dress was made by a guess," he had complained to close friends the day before. "The American wouldn't try on the gown and I have no idea whether it will fit or not."

These complaints had been accompanied by an ardent gesture that communicated his anger. But on this morning, he greeted the princess with a formal bow and a delightful smile. He would later tell everyone he knew how wonderfully gracious the princess had been. For the moment, he had a job to do—any alterations to the gown would have to be done within the hour. He fidgeted until the three ladies-in-waiting held the dress before Aleta and she stepped into it.

"Stand aside. *Allez, allez,*" the frustrated designer commanded the ladies. He buttoned the sixty-eight buttons that ran from the bottom of the gown to the top. He pulled the tulle train into place and scattered a row of servants who stood near the princess. He arranged the veil and pulled at the dress, this way and that, in order to get just the right effect.

Then, with the trepidation of all his years in the business, he stood in front of the princess and opened his eyes.

The dress fit perfectly.

"I am a genius!" he declared, thinking of the adulation—and money!—that would come to his design house as a result of this latest triumph. "My dear, I am so pleased that you are so beautiful. It sets off the dress so well."

"Thank you." Aleta nodded. But her mind wasn't on the gown, or the flowers, or her bridesmaids as they rushed her to the carriage that would take her to the cathedral.

It was with her beloved, as it should be for every bride.

She waved dutifully to her new subjects, who crowded the streets, windows and overlooking balconies to wave their Monticello flags and the occasional American flag. Confetti flew from the rooftops as the carriage bearing the new princess passed. A million hurrahs and cheers greeted her from every direction.

At the cathedral, she was greeted by Rhoda, Carla and Maggie. They had ridden in the carriage directly in front of her. In the vestibule, while ladies-in-waiting fixed each of the women's gowns and trains, the friends hurriedly exchanged excited descriptions of all they had seen that morning.

At last the music began and the walk down the aisle was to begin. As Aleta walked at the arm of the American ambassador who would give her away in the name of his country, she looked straight ahead—ignoring the soaring music and the rich interior of the cathedral.

The path to the altar cleared as her three friends took their places at the side and the ambassador slipped away. The prince took her into his arms and when her eyes met his, she had the confirmation that she had hoped for this morning.

The night before, she had been in the arms of the man she loved. And she could only hope that it had not been a mere dream.

The dream of the nine-year-old and her mother at an American grocery checkout line had come true, had become real.

She was a princess now.

And the dream of a young woman to be married to the man she loved had also come true.

She was a wife now.

And so much more.

Epilogue

(MONTICELLO)—Princess Aleta of Monticello and ten-day-old heir to the throne, Joseph Hortensio, were greeted by a crowd of well-wishers as they left the private hospital with proud pop, Prince Giancarlo. Joseph, weighing in at seven pounds, eight ounces, has guaranteed the future for the tiny principality.

The queen is said to be delighted at the birth of her first grandson and *Snoop* sources tell us that she is contemplating abdicating in favor of Giancarlo at the earliest opportunity.

Snoop sources also tell us that, unlike some other royal marriages that we keep our readers informed of, this marriage between commoner and royalty is here to stay! The bad-boy prince has mended his ways and we think—confidentially, of course—that the princess is just grand!

* * * * *

HE'S MORE THAN A MAN, HE'S ONE OF OUR

Fabulous Fathers

Dear Christina,

Stationed here in the Gulf, as part of the peacekeeping effort, I've learned that family and children are the most important things about life. I need a woman who wants a family as much as I do....

Love, Joe

Dear Joe,

How can I tell you this...?

Love, Christina

Dear Reader,
Read between the lines as Toni Collins's FABULOUS FATHER, Joe Parish, and Christina Holland fall in love through the mail in LETTERS FROM HOME. Coming this October from

Silhouette

R O M A N C E™

FFATHER2

Silhouette
R O M A N C E™

═══ **HEARTLAND HOLIDAYS** ═══

Christmas bells turn into wedding bells for the Gallagher siblings in Stella Bagwell's *Heartland Holidays* trilogy.

THEIR FIRST THANKSGIVING (#903) in November
Olivia Westcott had once rejected Sam Gallagher's proposal—and in his stubborn pride, he'd refused to hear her reasons why. Now Olivia is back…and it is about time Sam Gallagher listened!

THE BEST CHRISTMAS EVER (#909) in December
Soldier Nick Gallagher had come home to be the best man at his brother's wedding—not to be a groom! But when he met single mother Allison Lee, he knew he'd found his bride.

NEW YEAR'S BABY (#915) in January
Kathleen Gallagher had given up on love and marriage until she came to the rescue of neighbor Ross Douglas . . . and the newborn baby he'd found on his doorstep!

Come celebrate the holidays with Silhouette Romance!

HEART

Take 4 bestselling love stories FREE

Plus get a FREE surprise gift!

Special Limited-time Offer

Mail to Silhouette Reader Service™

In the U.S.	In Canada
3010 Walden Avenue	P.O. Box 609
P.O. Box 1867	Fort Erie, Ontario
Buffalo, N.Y. 14269-1867	L2A 5X3

YES! Please send me 4 free Silhouette Romance™ novels and my free surprise gift. Then send me 6 brand-new novels every month, which I will receive months before they appear in bookstores. Bill me at the low price of $2.25* each—a savings of 44¢ apiece off the cover prices. There are no shipping, handling or other hidden costs. I understand that accepting the books and gift places me under no obligation ever to buy any books. I can always return a shipment and cancel at any time. Even if I never buy another book from Silhouette, the 4 free books and the surprise gift are mine to keep forever.

*Offer slightly different in Canada—$2.25 per book plus 69¢ per shipment for delivery. Canadian residents add applicable federal and provincial sales tax. Sales tax applicable in N.Y.

215 BPA ADL9   315 BPA ADMN

Name _____ (PLEASE PRINT)

Address _____ Apt. No. _____

City _____ State/Prov. _____ Zip/Postal Code. _____

This offer is limited to one order per household and not valid to present Silhouette Romance™ subscribers. Terms and prices are subject to change.

SROM-92   © 1990 Harlequin Enterprises Limited

Silhouette
R O M A N C E™

★ WRITTEN IN THE STARS ★

WHEN A SCORPIO MAN MEETS A CANCER WOMAN

Luke Manning's broken heart was finally healed, and he vowed never to risk it again. So when this Scorpio man introduced himself to his neighbor, Emily Cornell, he had companionship on his mind—plain and simple. But just one look at the lovely single mom had Luke's pulse racing! Find out where friendship can lead in Kasey Michaels's PRENUPTIAL AGREEMENT, coming this November only from Silhouette Romance. It's WRITTEN IN THE STARS.